The Courtyard Children

The Courtyard Children

©Marija Poljak, 2020

Published by Rhiza Edge, 2020
An imprint of Rhiza Press
PO Box 1519,
Capalaba QLD 4159
Australia
www.rhizaedge.com.au

Cover design by Rhiza Press through Book Whispers
Layout by Rhiza Press

Print ISBN: 978-1-925563-96-2

A catalogue record for this
book is available from the
National Library of Australia

The Courtyard Children

MARIJA POLJAK

To my children

Od svog porijekla i djetinjstva ne može se lako pobjeći

'From one's ancestry and childhood, it is not easy to escape.'

- Ivo Andrić

Prologue

My *Dida* once said to me, *Living is hard, yet life is sweet.* I had never given it much thought as a child. Life was just life. Then everything happened, and I came to understand what my grandfather meant.

I picked up the book, my first ever gift from my first ever friend, and opened it to the first page. The blue ink had faded, leaving the inscription inside looking like a bland watercolour stain. But it was still legible. *To Mara. May 1980.*

His name was just a smudge beneath my own, but I never feared I would forget it. His name, like so many things, still haunted me on nights when I would awaken inexplicably from my dreams, and it came to me on days when I would unexpectedly catch a glimpse of beauty in the world; the spray of sea water crashing onto the pier, or a glint of sunshine splashed across an old façade, almost resurrecting what was lost long ago.

My well-read and much-loved copy of *The Little Prince* was beyond resurrection, but I would happily let each page crumble and slip away if it meant I could still keep that first one. That ordinary, yellowish nothingness of a page, which held but a few blotchy words, was worth so much more to me than the author's. The book was just an object now; a vessel for my memories.

It sat on my bookshelf, nestled among countless other books, each as inconsequential as the next. I did not want it isolated somewhere in the depths of the house. It sat here, in my presence, and on days like this—when I would find myself alone and with the house to myself—I would take *The Little Prince* gently into my hands and remember.

The courtyard. Standing together. His smile.

And then I would falter, and the feelings would come rushing in again, unabashed and unstoppable. I would be consumed by love and loss, grief and hope. And this time, like every other time, I would put the book back in its place.

Then I'd think of my own place, once upon a time.

I'm from a place where the sea cries when the sun refuses to shine, where the winds coming down from the mountains bring either relief or retribution, where pinecones sing like crickets during the heat and pine leaves fly like birds during the cold.

I am from perhaps the only place where blood is *not* thicker than water, as I have seen how we spill our own blood in the fight over every shoreline, river and bleak canal that runs through our troubled land.

My place may have forgotten me. But I am still here.

Chapter 1

The first few weeks of my life I had been known simply as *beba*—the baby. It went on like this until someone, my father I believe, suggested I be given a name. He argued that although *beba* was perfectly suitable for this stage of my life, it would only be a matter of time before I outgrew the title. Unless I was to be referred to as *the toddler, the child, the teenager, the adult* and eventually *the elderly woman*, it was essential that I be given a permanent name. It was at that moment my father recommended the name *Mileva*. He and my mother agreed and finally named me, and I took on the name of Albert Einstein's former wife.

One day, when I was much older, I asked my father why he chose to name me not after a genius, but the wife of a genius.

He tilted his head while looking at me and said, 'What, would you prefer the name *Albert*?' I considered it then shook my head. 'And anyway,' he continued. 'She *was* the brains in the relationship. You'd do well to do the same.'

Nonetheless, *Mileva* was rarely used, my parents preferring the nickname of *Mara*. I thus became known as Mara Marinković—a name I felt could belong to a children's cartoon character. You know, the kind that wore a costume and led a double life of fighting crime.

The reality of my life was much less exciting.

The use of such simplistic alliteration in my name had led the neighbourhood children to believe that I, myself, was a simpleton, and that my parents knew only half the letters of the alphabet. I thought this a very drastic conclusion to make from those who were *actually* barely familiar with the alphabet. Nonetheless, it led to a lot of '*Stara Mara, velika joj glava.*' *Old Mara, her head is large.* I didn't feel it was the best they could do, but it was enough. From then on, the size of my head became the focus of my worries.

My father, despite his questionable tactics, always had good intentions. Upon hearing my complaints about being taunted, he asked me, 'But you do know why you have a large head, don't you?' I looked at him blankly, waiting for the part where he made me feel better. 'It's because you have such a large brain!' he answered. And with a soft pat on my head and a kiss on the cheek, he smiled at me and went back to reading the newspaper. I stood alone, barely comforted by the fact that my own father had just confirmed the largeness of my head and had gone even further as to insult my brain.

So, I decided to take matters into my own hands. I moved on from concerning myself with the size of my head and instead chose to dedicate myself to one thing: *revenge.*

The courtyard of our apartment building was a combination of overgrown grass and gravel, which served as a makeshift parking lot. As such, it was often the cause of badly scraped knees and gravel-burn. I had been the victim of some serious gravel-burn myself—to this day, I have an unevenly coloured patch of skin on my right elbow to testify to the fact. Yet the courtyard was also a place of excitement and entertainment, for it was the meeting point for all the neighbourhood children.

The apartment block we lived in was long and unoriginal, set up in a U-shape with the outsides facing the surrounding streets. The courtyard was placed in the middle of the block, where mothers and fathers could watch their children from the windows facing inwards of any given apartment. Such buildings were a bastion in the design of socialist architecture, creating a sense of unity yet no specific identity. It also worked to the advantage of parents to whom surveillance was a priority.

Standing in the middle of the courtyard, one could do a 360-degree turn and have a direct insight into all the lives behind the windows. Women hunched over on their cramped balconies, yelling at their grandchildren below. Old men sitting in front of garage doors, either smoking cigarettes and debating politics, football or the price of seafood, or smoking cigarettes and playing *briškule*, whilst debating politics, football or the price of seafood. At other times one could catch movements behind the curtains of a window. And every so often some poor child's mother poking her head out of a window yelling at her son or daughter to come back up to the apartment – for the last time, she won't say it again, and she better not have to come down there, or 'just wait until your father gets home'. And although very rare, it was known to happen on occasion in the dimness of the late night that a couple might just start to get better acquainted with each other. This could go on for some time before the couple realised they had an audience of all the neighbourhood gathered.

Most of the time, the passionate couples would draw the curtains before anything of real interest happened. But the apartments were large and the families were many, so slip-ups were inevitable. None of us would ever forget the time when old Mr and Mrs Petrović had not only forgotten to close their curtains but had also left their window *wide open*.

It was in the courtyard that some of the most notable experiences had taken place, from the very good to the very bad, to the very scary. And it was here where I, at the age of seven, had decided to take revenge on those who thought it funny to make fun of, what I deemed, a perfectly normal-sized head. I set my sights on the ringleader—it was a well-known courtyard fact that taking down the leader would silence the herd.

His name was Marko, and I hated him.

I hated his crew-cut blond hair, his untrustworthy blue eyes, the way he wore sneakers without socks. But most of all, I hated when he teased me.

Marko lived in an apartment directly parallel to mine; we were at opposite ends of the U-shape, facing each other but separated by the large courtyard below. My family lived on the third level, and so did his. He and I were even the same age, and, with school approaching, I knew I had to do something about this kid before we ended up in the same class where he could humiliate me further.

My mother was one of those mothers who always repeated to her daughter, 'You know that boy is only teasing you because he likes you.' Adults often have the most confusing way of interpreting others' actions. In my generosity, I forgave my mother because I knew that in her old age, she had just lost touch with the minds of children.

Instead, I planned to publicly ridicule Marko to make him aware of our status as mortal enemies.

When not in the courtyard, the children of our apartment block would often be found down at the beach, accompanied by whosever parent's turn it was to keep an eye on all of us. Fortunately for me, on a particularly fine day of summer when I was due to carry out my revenge, we were enlisted in the care of rosy-faced Ana's grandfather.

Ana was a girl whose face was always rosy. Her grandfather, though, was even rosier-faced—although none of us really knew why, since all he ever did was sit outside of his garage and drink *rakija* all day. I thanked my luck that he had summoned the strength to take us kids down to the beach, for I could not have hoped for a less attentive carer.

I must admit that even I had succumbed to the sheer joy of a simple, sunny day in summer—one of the remaining few before we were to set off to school for the first time. I could not blame myself for forgetting my revenge plot momentarily; with the sun not going down until well into the evening, I spent the entire afternoon in a state of saltiness and warmth.

The soles of my feet were strong after a summer of being hardened by the small and roughened stones that lined our beaches. It never did take long to get used to that uneven surface beneath my feet. Our mothers always made sure to make us wear our rubber sandals for fear of stepping on a *jež*, but the unwatchful eye of Ana's grandfather meant that we could easily avoid any semblance of safety on this day.

It wasn't until I was staring at a spiky sea urchin clinging to the rocky pier that I was reminded of my revenge plan. And, seeing the perfect opportunity, I was quick to act. Unaware, Marko had run off behind a stall in order to get changed out of his wet swimming shorts. Thinking fast, I grabbed the sea urchin gently as possible, and then two more on my way out of the water. Resting them in the palms of my hands, I arranged them in a row outside the exit of the stall. Then, in my moment of brilliance, I swiped Marko's dry clothes that were hanging over the top of the stall.

As I quickly sprinted off, I heard someone shout, 'Hey!' Dashing out of the stall was Marko, with his towel wrapped around his waist and trying to catch whoever had just played that dirty prank on him. Even I had forgotten about the sea urchins I had placed on the ground, right up until Marko stepped directly onto one of them, letting out a tremendous scream. My stomach turned as I heard him yell, but the feeling of unease was made even worse when Marko began to hop on one foot and stepped hard onto the tip of his towel, yanking it straight off his waist and onto the ground.

Any feelings of unease or brief regret escaped me, as I, along with all the other children on the beach, erupted into fits of laughter. Marko, amazingly enough, was not as embarrassed as he was hurt. I thought he was somehow managing to ignore the surrounding onslaught of laughter, but it soon became clear that he was beginning to comprehend the magnitude of the situation. With the laughter subsiding and my fear of retribution growing, I quickly ran up to him and said, 'Marko! Here are your clothes!'

He took them somewhat sheepishly and pulled on his shorts, muttering a quiet, 'Thanks.'

I suppose all the noise must have roused Ana's grandfather, who up until that point was having a nice nap in the late afternoon sun. He came to us, even redder in the face than usual, telling us to stop the noise and that it's time to go home.

Marko was sitting on the ground attempting to pull whatever sea-urchin spikes he could from the sole of his foot. I sat down and struggled to help him, knowing all too well that our efforts were futile—Marko would simply have to wait for his body to reject the painful spikes.

He soon got up to go home, and, hobbling on one leg, said, 'Thanks, Mara. Thanks for giving me my clothes when no one else would.'

I didn't have the heart to tell him it was I who had taken the clothes in the first place. And fortunately, no one ever did reveal the truth. But from that day forward, for whatever reason, we became the closest of friends.

Many years later, when I confessed to him that I had been his undoing, he told me he had known all along.

When not at home, I, like most children my age, would spend my days with my grandparents. My memories before I started school consisted mostly of summers by the sea, often up north in the *selo*, and spring days spent in the green fields of *Lika*. Life was divided between the two mountainsides; the inland forests and the rocky coast. Occasionally, we would take trips to *Beli Zagreb Grad* or to the mountains of *Jahorina*, where surrounding villages still resembled Ottoman ideals.

My father's mother lived in an apartment quite close to ours. Having dedicated much of her life to work, she was enjoying the benefits of an early retirement that many other people still had to wait years to reach. However, this also made her the prime candidate for child-minding. Baka Roza often used this situation as an opportunity to state that she had already 'had her turn' at raising children. (Or at raising *one child*, as my mother always liked to whisper under her breath).

She would come to care for me at our apartment, so that I was kept occupied in my bedroom with my toys, and she could feed me with the food from our kitchen rather than wasting her own. Baka Roza had been a bit of a scrooge, but my father always defended her by arguing that she had survived two World Wars and had thus developed a habit of being industriously thrifty. Once, when I snapped a rubber band and went to throw it in the bin, Baka Roza took it from me and tied the ends back together, claiming it was still perfectly fine to use.

'You don't know what it's like to have no food in the kitchen, Mara,' my father would tell me. 'And you are lucky, because in *this* country, you will never go hungry.'

My father, Lazar, was named after a famous Tsar who led the Battle of Kosovo. Tata did well to grow into his name, for he had joined the army immediately after completing high school and his sense of patriotism kept him there.

To say that my grandmother was immensely and nauseatingly proud of her only son would be a glorious understatement. He was the only human being alive with the power to change my grandmother's mind. He had his mother's eyes; a deep blue-green colour. But unlike his mother, who was fair and blonde, my father bore thick, dark hair, and skin much darker than any of ours. He appeared heavily tanned. And if he hadn't kept his hair cut short in line with army expectations, it would have enveloped his entire head.

My Baka Roza, although full of love, provided nowhere near enough excitement a child my age was hoping for. I was therefore always secretly pleased when my parents announced to me that they would be taking me to Lika to stay with my mother's parents. Lika was like a wonderland for children. It was nothing but amazing expanses of green fields, large trees, plants and flowers of all kinds, stunning lakes and creeks. My grandparents in Lika were also far more lenient than city-folk, and they saw no problem with me running around the wilderness and getting caked in dirt. 'If anything, it will only help strengthen her immune system,' my Baka Anka would say.

Chapter 2

During the last summer before I was to start school, my parents decided to send me to Lika for a whole fifteen days. On the day of departure, Mama, as always, packed my bags for me as though I was embarking on a journey to conquer Mount Everest. This was not unusual. Although my father still rolled his eyes at her, reminding her that if I could sleep for eight hours without food every single night, then I could surely survive a two-hour car journey.

Still, after a three-course lunch and much hugging and kissing, Mama waved Tata and I goodbye, and we sat in our blue Fiat and headed for Lika. Tata let me sit in the passenger seat, which I was very proud of. Though, it may have had something to do with the back seat being taken up by a large sports bag containing all of my clothes (including several jumpers because you know how cold it can get over there, even in summer), two large grocery bags that were packed with salami and prosciutto sandwiches with cheese, two bottles of water, three apples, a container of fried capsicums, a thermos of hot rose-hip tea and a small packet of *Plazma* biscuits. In my hand, I had a savoury bread roll covered in salt and a carton of juice.

My father rolled down the windows while I waved goodbye to my mother through the back window. Some of the other neighbourhood kids who were running around the courtyard soon turned their attention to our departing vehicle, chasing it out onto the road and repeatedly yelling, *'Ćao, ćao!'*

I saw Marko running around with them, and he pulled a face, sticking out his tongue as we drove off.

'Who's that little punk?' Tata asked, grinning to himself.

'Nobody important,' I replied.

On the road, my father and I would play games. It always started with something basic; he would pick a colour (usually red) and I would pick another (usually white). Every time a car of our chosen colour drove past us in the opposite direction, we would get a point. I seemed to always win, and my father would say it was because I was smart enough to pick a common colour for cars. He said he liked that I was so logical in my thinking, whatever that meant. We would then advance to the next game: guessing colours. Once we hit an open stretch of road and could not see any cars approaching us, we would have to guess the colour of the next car that was to drive by. Whoever got it right would win yet another point.

'White!' I called out, seeing a car far off in the distance and readying myself for victory. Tata just laughed.

'Very creative,' he said. 'Ok then, red.' A car came around the bend and drove past us. It was blue.

'Tata, let's play another game,' I asked. 'This one's getting boring.'

'Yes, I agree,' he said. 'How about this: I will say a word, and you must say another word beginning with the letter that my word ended in.'

'What?' I said. He smiled to himself.

'If I say the word *road*, what letter does *road* end in?' he asked me. As a seven-year-old, I gave it some thought.

'It ends in *d*!'

'That's right! So, what's a word beginning with the letter *d*?'

'Dog!' I yelled.

12

'Exactly, now you get it,' he said to me. 'Okay, I will then say ... goat!'

'Hmm ... truck?'

'Yes, very good. You're a natural at this game, Mara!'

We exhausted a good half an hour of the ride playing the same game, and it would get harder and harder as my father used more obscure and complicated words. I could not seem to get past the basics, but he was proud of me for always coming up with a word, whatever it was. It was not until I had to think of a word beginning with the letter *b* and called out 'baby' that the game finally ended and the topic changed.

'Speaking of babies,' my father said, 'how would you like it if you were to have a little brother or sister?'

He said this so suddenly and with such ease that it caught me by surprise. I looked up at Tata with excitement. Years ago, he and Mama always used to ask me if I would like a little brother or sister. The answer was always yes, of course, but a sibling never arrived. After a while they stopped asking me and I did not ask them either, and as my Baka Anka always told me, I will only get a brother or sister 'if it's God's will.'

'What do you mean?' I asked my father. 'Are you saying I'm going to have one? For real this time?'

Tata cast me a sideways glance, the corners of his mouth curving upwards ever so slightly.

'Your mother and I didn't want to say anything to you until we could be certain,' my father told me. 'Well, we're certain now. You will have your brother or sister in a few month's time.'

I could only look at my father with the goofiest smile on my face as I thought about what it would mean to be a big sister. I had to be responsible now. I would have to teach my sibling everything: how to tie shoelaces, how to count to one hundred. I would be the one walking him or her to school every day.

'I'm glad you're happy, Mara,' my father said. 'I'm happy, too.'

The remainder of the trip was spent in rushed conversation, as my father patiently tolerated the barrage of questions I sent his way.

'Can I choose the baby's name? Where will the baby sleep? Can it sleep in my room? When can we go buy toys for the baby? Can I help Mama dress the baby?'

'Yes. Not sure yet. Perhaps. Soon. Sure,' Tata said. It was no secret that I had been waiting for this moment, although I am sure that my parents were even more relieved than I was. I was too young to have known of my parents' troubles, to have even considered the possibility that they had difficulty conceiving, that my own existence was seen as a miracle. And that is why, after seven years of my life, I found it perfectly normal (and about time, really), that I was soon to be a big sister.

I could not wait to see Baka Anka and Dida Ilija, to tell them the good news. Arriving in Lika was like entering a whole new realm; greenery and grass replaced the earthy colours and stones of the coastal land that I was used to. The sky opened up before us and was broken on the horizon – not by the sea, but by great hills and forests. This is the place I associated with wild animals, with freezing winters and pleasant summers, delicious and hearty food, and cool drinks of Baka's homemade lemonade.

We pulled into the driveway of my grandparents' old home and I rushed out of the Fiat before my father could even park it properly. The first to greet me was the dog – Ninja. I had found him a few years ago wandering aimlessly and alone in the park by the marina as a puppy. He was a mixed-breed of sorts, about medium-build with soft brown hairs. Completely unremarkable in every way, but I loved him from the start. I had fed him some lollies that day in the park and from that moment on, he was reluctant to leave my side. My mother just about had a heart attack when she saw him run out from under my bed one day (after I had managed to sneak him into our apartment).

Needless to say, I was not allowed to keep him. But my onslaught of tears must have plucked at my parents' heartstrings just enough, for they gave in and managed to negotiate an agreement with my grandparents to have the dog stay in Lika. In honour of the dog's perseverance and of his sneaky ability to creep into our lives with such stealth, I named him Ninja.

Upon seeing me, Ninja immediately threw himself at my feet and assumed the submissive position of lying on his back and sticking out his belly, which I gave a good scratch. I wondered why people could not always be so glad to see each other, but my mind changed somewhat when I saw my Baka Anka come towards me, embracing me in one of those extreme grandmother-style hugs. She planted about a dozen kisses on my face before my Dida Ilija could finally get close, and I jumped into his arms as though he were as fit as my young father, rather than an elderly man. Dida never complained though.

For all the talking I did with my father, I did the opposite with my grandfather. Between us existed only silence, at least on my part. He and I had some sort of unspoken alliance and a common enemy in my parents, and I will always be grateful for the stories Dida shared with me about my mother—these stories served as important ammunition against her to be brought up at a future date.

Having gone deaf towards the end of World War Two, Dida Ilija was a man who had to learn to adapt. A new world was growing and new countries were being born; borders were changing, as were attitudes. For a deaf man, there were no words to explain new ideas or new objects. Life became about attaching labels to certain things, in order to retain a sense of familiarity. Ilija had to take what he already knew and apply it to what he did not know.

When the Second World War was ending, the planes overhead began to change. It was no longer bombs that were being dropped, but deliveries of aid packages. It was no longer the Germans or the Ustashe flying overhead, but the Americans and our allies. And with the arrival of the Americans came the arrival of bananas. Never before had this man from Lika seen bananas. This exotic fruit was unlike anything else grown or eaten in Lika.

For the rest of his life, Ilija would not know that bananas were bananas. How could he hear what they were called? How does a deaf man learn a word he has never heard of, belonging to an object he has never seen? And it did not help Dida Ilija that he was illiterate. So, upon having tried the mysterious new fruit, Ilija concluded that it most closely reminded him of one thing: potatoes. The fruit was soft and mushy like a cooked potato. But of course, it was not a potato. Not even close. Alas, the bananas were given the name of American potatoes.

I would use whatever sign language I could to try and communicate with him. When he spoke too loudly, I would lift my hand and move it downwards, to signify that he needed to control the volume of his voice. Sometimes he would become self-conscious and reduce his speech to barely a whisper, where upon I would raise my hand and cup it to my ear, to show him that he needed to speak up. Through practice he had come to master the right tone of voice and to speak at a reasonable volume, but sometimes outside noise would interfere, such as the neighbour firing up their tractor, and I would have to signal to Dida to speak up. He would look at me, somewhat bewildered, until I mimicked the action of someone riding a tractor. My Dida would grasp what I meant, and these explanations soon turned into frequent games of charades.

Dida Ilija would still enjoy eating American potatoes. He would ask me, '*Oko moje*, please bring me one of those American potatoes.' He called me *oko moje*, 'my eye', the centre of his world. He called me this because he had never heard or read my name. I called him 'Dida' even though I knew he could not hear me, but because he would always call himself that, most often when he would announce, 'Dida loves you,' as his way of saying goodbye. I would always bring him whatever he asked for and I would smile as I watched my grandfather savour the taste of an American potato.

Tata did not stay long in Lika for he had to return to be with my mother. He stayed long enough to have some coffee and *burek* with his in-laws, and to discuss the good news he had shared with me during our car journey; that the baby was due to come towards the end of the year.

My father came and gave me a big hug before he left. It was late in the afternoon, but he would arrive home before nightfall— the benefit of long summer days. Dida Ilija helped my father load up the boot of the car with some necessities. Fresh fruits and vegetables—whatever was in season—some large eggs from Baka's reliable chickens and some *slanina* from the previous winter that my grandfather had smoked himself in the shed by the house. The neighbour had brought over some goat's cheese and Baka Anka made a point of saying how well it would serve my mother during her pregnancy. I for one hated goat's cheese and was happy to see Baka unload it all upon my father.

Tata winked at me as he started up the car, the windows all rolled down. 'Be good,' he said. 'I'll see you soon, *princezo*.'

He turned the car around and drove down the driveway, honking the car horn as he turned right onto the road. Ninja ran after him, down the gravel driveway, stopping finally when he got onto the road.

'So,' Baka said. 'Who's hungry?' This was, as always, a rhetorical question, where it is assumed the answer is only ever, 'I am!'

I followed Baka into the house, the smell of hot food wafting through every room making me forget any absence of appetite I may have had. I knew what was for lunch before I even got to the kitchen from the unmistakable scent; *sarma* and freshly baked bread on the side. Baka always made it with mashed potatoes, because she knew that was how I liked it best. For dessert, one of my favourite dishes: apple *pita*, still in the oven, but just about ready.

I sat at the kitchen table next to Dida Ilija, who was sipping on some Turkish coffee. I loved the smell of that coffee, but on the single occasion where I tried it, it was enough to put me off the taste. I presumed it was one of those things adults made themselves drink even if they did not like the taste—kind of like beer and *rakija*.

Baka Anka had already set the table and was dishing out generous servings of *sarma* for all of us. Her timing was impeccable as always for food delivery; she had a sixth sense that knew exactly when I would turn up, so the food would always be *just* finished and ready to eat. This was another skill I assumed only developed in adults, or maybe only in grandmothers.

I ate my lunch as question after question from Baka assailed me, and in between the mouthfuls of *sarma* and mashed potatoes I could hardly get a word in. When I did attempt to answer one of Baka's questions, she would immediately intervene with, 'No, no, you mustn't speak with your mouth full. Just finish your food first.' Thus, lunch carried on in such a way that Baka barely ate any food at all, I ate my food in confusion, and Dida finished his meal long before the rest of us. He then proceeded to look at me, rolling his eyes at the sight of Baka's ceaseless mouth.

In the late afternoon it was still much too hot to go and play outside, and Baka did not want to risk me getting heatstroke. Even Ninja was lying on the porch in the shade provided by the grapevines, looking very satisfied with life. Dida Ilija came and sat next to me, holding some sort of wooden box.

'Come,' he said, almost in a whisper. 'You are about to start school. It is time you learned how to play chess.'

I sat up, intrigued. The wooden box had black and white squares on top of it, and when Dida slid it open it revealed all the chess pieces inside, also carved from wood.

Baka was standing close to us, watching, as she ironed the clothes that had been packed in my suitcase. Mama always packed my clothes so well that they did not need to be ironed, but Baka always ironed them anyway. How she could stand to do this in the paralysing heat was unimaginable to me, but she insisted that no granddaughter of hers would be running around in creased clothing for everyone to see.

'Now,' Dida Ilija said. 'All of these ones here, they are called pawns. Understand?'

I nodded and furrowed my brow.

'Good,' he continued. He went on to list the remaining pieces, until he reached the final one. 'This one here is the most important,' he said. 'This is the queen. And the queen ... she can do anything.' I looked at the piece he held in his hand, attempting to forge to my memory the image of this most significant of chess pieces.

'Chess is like a metaphor for life, *oko moje*,' my Dida said to me. 'It is the man—the king—who is seen as the most important, who is meant to be the leader. But it is really the woman by his side who has all the power and does all she can to protect him. She holds it all together.' Dida Ilija had reduced his voice almost to a whisper by this point, yet I looked at him intently. I nodded to indicate that I understood. I knew once I started playing the game—and I was very eager by now—that it would all become more confusing than it seemed.

'Always be a queen, *oko moje*,' said my Dida, louder now. 'Don't you ever be a pawn.'

Chapter 3

It was the spring of 1978 when I started school. Expectations were high, and I volunteered to give the first presentation in class about a chosen family member.

I stood up and began with, 'My dad.' I spoke about my father, and I spoke well.

I spoke with the confidence of a child who is sure of the world around her. The teacher—a kind and supportive woman—listened. She nodded when she had to. She smiled at me at the right times. I continued, speaking about my father.

I talked about how he would take me to football matches that he would referee, and I would sit in the players' box of the home team and give them advice on the match. I talked about the time my father taught me how to swim, up north in the *selo*, by throwing me into the sea and saying, 'swim.' I talked about how, on one occasion a few weeks ago, he drove us across the state border, deciding that we would spend the weekend in his hometown simply to recall his childhood there.

I continued my talk. I talked about my father's dark, wavy hair, his blue eyes and his large, engulfing arms. I mentioned that he rarely drank but he loved to celebrate. He was always generous with guests and there was always plenty of food and *rakija*. He was talkative and energetic, but extremely calm and wise. He was well-read and intelligent, and a dedicated army officer. He loved his country (the teacher smiled approvingly at this statement). As I summarised my talk, I grew more confident and was quite happy with myself. I felt I had described my father well and that I had pleased my teacher, too.

'And finally,' I said, wrapping up my talk, 'my dad, just like you, Miss, is fat. Thank you!' Feeling triumphant, I took my seat to the sound of applause and cheering from my peers, foolishly believing they were in awe of my talk when in fact they were simply in awe of my bravery, which I was yet to be made aware of.

The talk I then received from the teacher was perhaps more memorable than the talk I had made to the class. It was there that I learnt that honesty was not always valued, despite my having been taught to always be honest. It was also then that I learnt how my teacher had a genetic condition and she was not *really* fat, not like the way a person who eats too much food is fat, anyway. At that age, I was not sure why she was telling me this, but I suppose she felt it an important thing to clarify. Either way, her size was of no significance to me, but I liked that she reminded me of my chubby father.

My next school assignment, carrying on from the talk we had given about a chosen family member, was to research our family history and draw up a family tree. The teacher gave each student a large piece of paper with a tree already drawn onto it; the branches had lines on them where we were to write the names of our ancestors. I was looking forward to this task very much, if not only to redeem myself for my previous blunder.

I filled out as much as I could of my family tree, but there were still gaps. On my mother's side I added her older sister and younger brother, but I struggled to go beyond my grandparents and even had to stop at the name of Tata's father. I had never known him; I did not even know his name, so I thought it best to discuss this with Baka Roza.

She was incredibly excited that I had started school and was always eager to help me with any work. She was all the more delighted to have the opportunity to discuss her past, and, as with any brief conversation with Baka Roza, I ended up on the receiving end of the passionate retelling of her life story.

When my Baka Roza was a child (she began by telling me), she became a victim of the Spanish influenza. This particular strain of the flu had killed more people during World War One than the actual war itself. However, my grandmother survived. She overcame the flu, and from then onwards, never got sick again. But it scared her enough that she promised to herself she would never have children and have to go through what her mother went through.

Then the Second World War came and went, resulting in an inconceivable loss of human life. And, as my grandmother explained, something about that makes a person 'really think about things'. And I guess she must have thought pretty hard, because she decided to have my father.

But Baka Roza never said much beyond that. All I knew about my grandfather was that he came from a small Bosnian Muslim family who lived south-east, in the town where my father was born. When my father was only nine years of age, his father died. Not long after, my father and Baka Roza returned to Dalmatia.

I never had much contact with my grandfather's side of the family. Tata would tell me stories of his father, but his own paternal grandparents had died long ago. All Tata knew was that his grandmother was a Romi woman and his grandfather a tailor. They only had the one son, my unknown grandfather, Emir, whose name I included on my family tree.

It was during moments of great dissatisfaction with life that I imagined the grandiose return of an unknown family member from my father's estranged side. They'd reappear—bearing a striking resemblance to myself—to announce the revival of our royal and respectable family, who would finally rise again to our position of societal prominence after years spent defeating rival armies and dissidents. This, of course, never occurred. To dream of ancestral royalty was idealistic for most people, let alone a descendant of a poor Romi and a common tailor. Instead, I could only hope to prove to the masses that a child of such mixed heritage could contribute as much as anyone to maintaining *brotherhood and unity*.

Despite her reluctance to reveal the details of her private life involving my late Dida Emir and his family, my Baka Roza was eager to discuss her own family's past; that much, she knew. 'You need to know who your ancestors were, Mara,' she would tell me. 'You need to know who they were, so that you may know who *you* are.' She had captured my curiosity enough for me to hear her out.

'You are a Marinković. A long time ago, around the time of the Battle of Kosovo, our name nearly disappeared. It was at the time that the Turks were occupying our land and had begun sending their soldiers further and further into our kingdom as the war spread. At first, the villagers were cooperative. Our family allowed them to take some food, to have somewhere to stay the night. But then the soldiers asked too much. They began to demand our possessions, and, worst of all, our women. This is when the men in the family had enough, and they killed the several soldiers who were stationed in our village, disposing of their bodies.'

My mouth was hanging open, as though it was trying to swallow every word my grandmother said. I urged her, with my eyes, to continue.

'No one thought anything of it; it was as though the soldiers had disappeared into thin air ... but our own village rivalries proved to be our undoing. One evening in the local inn, a young Marinković woman got into an argument with another local woman. Some Turkish soldiers who were passing through happened to overhear the women's bitter exchange of words. It was not of any particular importance, until the second woman shouted, "What are you going to do? Kill me and throw my body into the river like your family did to all those Turk soldiers? Ha!" The Marinković woman waved it off, but the soldiers paid full attention.'

I wiped the bit of drool that was escaping from my still-open mouth.

'You can imagine what happened next. It was not long before the Turkish soldiers reported the gossip back to their commanders further east. They could not have the deaths of their own go unpunished. Soon after the incident in the local inn, a swarm of Turkish soldiers descended upon the village, with the intention of avenging their comrades' deaths. They methodically found every Marinković in the village and killed them. No one was exempt, from old to young.'

A short squeal escaped my mouth.

'But,' my grandmother added, 'it was not quite the end. There were some survivors, one in particular: the young woman, the one whose conflict in the inn had started it all. And, as luck had it, she was pregnant with a child. A boy. She ended up leaving the village, along with several other families who felt it safer to move. She had her boy and he went on to have three more boys of his own. Those boys and their descendants were the first to settle and help establish the villages that lie beneath Velebit. Our *selo* was one of them. And now, many, many generations later … here you are.'

I smiled at Baka Roza. Roza Marinković, who gave birth to a son and gave him *her* family's name.

The day after the national celebrations of the 29th of November, my family continued celebrating, for we welcomed a new life into our household. In the late evening, my little sister screamed her way into this world. The nurses at the hospital could not help but comment on the lush dark hair she was born with, or the large, inquisitive green eyes. Nor could they resist saying that never before had they seen a father so happy to receive a daughter.

I remember being in the waiting room with Tata, for no one else was allowed to be present during the actual birth. My father was not happy about having to wait outside and he made no secret of the fact. He was proving to be quite the distraction to the nurses on staff. Right up until my Baka Anka showed up.

'Where is she? Where is my daughter?!' she wailed dramatically as she strode into the waiting room.

One of the nurses told her that my mother was already in labour and that visitors must wait outside.

'What?!' my grandmother called out. 'No, no, I must be there, I must do this for her! Please, *Bože*, let me give birth instead of her! Let me undergo the suffering, spare my daughter this pain!'

The nurse rolled her eyes and instructed my grandmother to please sit down. Tata calmed down Baka Anka enough so she would take a seat beside him. It was too late for me, however. My grandmother's antics were enough to terrify me, and I imagined all sorts of terrible things occurring in that little room where my mother was experiencing such agony. I almost wished that Baka Anka *could* take Mama's place.

Fortunately, I only had to bear a few more minutes of my grandmother's whimpering and my father's unrelenting foot-tapping until it was finally over.

A nurse entered the waiting room and announced that my sister had been born after an uncomplicated labour. I practically felt the air in the room lighten, the tension released from the atmosphere and from those around me.

As promised to me by Tata, I was to name my sibling. I chose the name *Alisa*. I had her future mentally mapped out in my mind, and it consisted only of great happiness and immeasurable success. I looked at the miniature version of my parents, a version of myself, too, but with light eyes where mine were dark and dark hair where mine was light. She was perfect. And she was mine.

At home, Dida Ilija was waiting for us. He smiled so hard at the good news that his face almost cracked along his wrinkle lines. He and Baka Anka stayed for a few days more, at least enough to see Mama and Alisa settle in back home. Within the first week of December though, they had to return to Lika. The weather was getting considerably cooler after all, and who knew how quickly the first snowstorm would come and block off all the roads leading out of town.

Baka Roza had regained a sense of purpose in her life. The doting grandmother once more, she was perhaps more present in our home than was necessary. Mama couldn't help but notice how Baka Roza's 'help' largely came in the form of cuddling the baby and planting kisses on her face, yet when the crying began or the nappies needed changing, Baka was already preparing to head off back to her apartment, 'not wanting to be a burden'.

'How considerate of her,' my mother muttered to me with a wink. I stifled a laugh, finding it all too amusing when one of my parents hinted a negative sentiment towards another family member. It felt so immoral, yet so satisfying. I loved seeing adults act this way. I eventually would grow to learn that this was not as uncommon as I thought; criticisms of family members were frequent, and I would experience time and again adults breaking the rules they so strongly sought to impose on children.

One afternoon when my mother and I were walking upstairs to our apartment after picking up some groceries, we ran into our middle-aged neighbour, who lived in the apartment below us. Mrs Lukić was also carrying groceries and my mother asked me to help her, at which Mrs Lukić smiled.

'But, Mama,' I protested. 'I think Mrs Lukić should carry all her stuff on her own, you said so yourself that she could use more exercise. Remember? You said she needs more exercise and less make-up!'

I was made to do all the chores that entire weekend, which my mother assured me was nothing compared to the shame I had put her through. I was no longer allowed to say *anything* about *anyone*, but my mother continued to bad-mouth whomever she considered worth bad-mouthing. It did not bother me so much. I would simply save all my opinions of others for when I became an adult and then it would be acceptable to say them out loud.

I could forgive my mother for her inconsistent expectations. She was clearly quite busy with my younger sister, so I imagined her brain wasn't working to its full potential. Mama stayed home with Alisa during the day, while I still had to go to school, braving the cold and the rain as I strolled through the streets and alleyways of town. In my mind I tried to overcome my confusions, wondering whether today I should be honest or whether I should be polite. Regardless of how hard I tried, though, I could never quite reconcile the two: honesty and politeness. What difficult demands the adult world imposed upon itself, I wondered, and could not help but be puzzled by all of it.

My journey to school was made much easier each day by the presence of Marko by my side, who, I must admit, was not as bad as I had thought. We had become a formidable pair, and it was nice knowing I had an ally in the school yard. He also made me feel better about myself. Marko had received a grade of two on his last assignment, which consisted of an elaborately made-up family tree containing ancestors with royal lineage, several notable tsars and even Genghis Khan. The teacher was clearly sceptical and chastised Marko for his lack of research but resolved not to fail him seeing as he had obviously put quite a lot of creative effort into his work. At least his iconic ancestors followed a chronological order on his family tree.

Ana was walked to school every day by her infamous grandfather, who, to our bewilderment, never faltered in waking right on time each morning and making sure his granddaughter arrived safely at her school, where he did not let her leave his sight until she walked through the main doors of the building. It was in class that I would finally take my seat next to her, because of course I could not be seen sitting next to Marko, a *boy*, all day long. Marko was immediately liked by just about all of the other school kids anyway, so he had his fair share of fans wanting to sit next to him.

Nikola was a saviour. Whenever I feared Marko was on the verge of idiocy, Nikola would come and save the day. How the two of them became best of friends, I would never know. Nikola was a soft-spoken boy with deep brown eyes, eyes that you could swim in. He had soft brown hair to match his eyes and his face never betrayed him by revealing anything sinister. He was painfully modest, perhaps due to his poor background.

As spoiled as Marko was, I had to give him credit for remaining fair towards Nikola. Marko never spoke down to him. But there was no ignoring the luxuries lacking in Nikola's life. Every day when we had a break at school to eat our food, Nikola would have a stale bread roll with very little meat in it.

One day, I asked Nikola why he only ever had stale bread to eat.

'My mum says we can't eat today's bread until we've eaten yesterday's, so I have to eat yesterday's bread first,' Nikola told me. 'Then tomorrow I will eat today's bread, and the fresh bread will wait for the day after. But by then it will be stale.' I didn't laugh because I felt so sad for him, but when Nikola began smiling, I realised it was okay to join in. Nikola didn't mind being trapped in a cycle of eating old bread, even if it didn't make much sense.

Nikola's family also lived in a large apartment block like ours, but unlike ours, theirs wasn't a proper apartment. They lived right at the bottom in what was the basement, so they didn't have any balconies or anything. They also had to share part of their space with all the other occupants, because the basement was really like a storeroom for everyone. My father had once explained to me how in our country everyone had a place to live, food to eat and clothes to wear. This made me happy and I had always believed it, right up until I met Nikola.

Nikola's father, Aco, had some sort of illness which slowly

destroyed his muscles. It meant that he had to stay home and only Nikola's mother, Vesna, could go to work. I found this really sad, too, but every time I saw Nikola's father, he was so full of laughter. He didn't seem sad at all. And their entire home was covered in amazing paintings that Aco had created. Sunsets, waves and all the colours of Dalmatia filled the walls of Nikola's small apartment with an artistry and finesse one might not expect from a man in Aco's condition. Nikola's little family was the epitome of resilience, and talent.

When I really thought about it, Nikola and his parents never complained. I only remember hearing his mother say once that she wished she could have had another child. But straight after she had said that one of Nikola was better than hundreds of others put together.

As school went on, Nikola served as the little angel hovering over Marko's right shoulder, always pleading with him to reconsider jumping across the desks, or sneaking out the window, or removing all the chairs from the classroom and hiding them in the school yard. He was like a weight on a set of scales, always seeking to provide a balance for whatever Marko was doing.

Ana was the observer, the one who stood by the sidelines until she saw fit to make herself known. She was less encouraging of Marko's antics than I was, which was probably for the better. Not that Marko needed much encouragement. I was a bit weaker than the others and found it hard to resist an opportunity for laughter. Marko had picked up on this—most of his acts of stupidity occurred when I was present in the audience, as though he needed to stage a performance for me.

We all got to know Marko's parents incredibly well thanks to their numerous visits to the school principal. Marko's mother was one of those angelic beings, soft-spoken to the point of being timid at times. She was always kind towards me and towards her son, which did not make her much of a disciplinarian. But I got the feeling that she was not entirely attuned to her son's tendencies towards misbehaviour, for Marko was always so composed when in her company.

Marko's father, on the other hand, was a frightening man. I had seen enough of him in the neighbourhood to notice his lack of tenderness. He would always address me when he came to our school, but he did so in a dismissive tone. He was not like his wife, who would look warmly into your eyes when speaking to you. Marko's father came across as impatient and anxious, as though he was judging each person he encountered.

If I had a father like Marko's, I would not dare put a toe out of line. But Marko took the opposite approach. The more his father reprimanded him, threatened him, and even hurt him, the less Marko tried to do what was right. He was a rebel from a young age, but such an attitude did not sit well with the mentality of our people and the system of our institutions. School was but the first hurdle for Marko, who would eventually find himself up against even greater obstacles in society. Yet no one cared to address the root of his problems and to consider why Marko was so resistant. No one saw what I saw—the life Marko had at home—and if people did know, they chose to ignore it. Admittedly, sometimes I was one of those people. Some things just weren't my business.

However, as different as we all might have been, we still made a close-knit group: Ana, Marko, Nikola and me. Whatever difficulties came our way, we suspected they would just as quickly disappear, and we would carry on living as we had always done; *fearlessly and as friends.*

Chapter 4

Under the glare of the summer sun, we drove to the *selo* where Baka Roza came from, and where her brother, Dmitar, still lived. He had an old house there perched on a hill, overlooking the sea. For the past few years my father had been helping his uncle refurbish the residence and make it at least somewhat liveable, so that we could visit more often. Up until then, Dmitar had been enjoying the company of owls and bats, who made their homes in the rafters of the roof. They had since left to make way for his human guests.

Dmitar was a man who had puzzled me in my younger years but began to make a lot more sense as I got older. He looked a lot like his sister but was quite different in character; far less obtrusive, and more subtle in his comments and mannerisms. He seemed more drawn to the simple life and claimed to be quite content in the village. Dmitar was the embodiment of a true Dalmatian. He cared only for the sea and the food that came from it and consumed olive oil as though it were water.

Baka Roza, as per usual, chose to stay in the comfort of her city apartment that summer rather than to venture back to her village of birth. Her brother was as stubborn as her, for he had opted to never leave *his* home. Thus, the siblings remained in their respective residencies and communicated via telephone. It was an odd arrangement, and it made me wonder about my sister and me. Alisa would always remain by my side, I knew that, and I certainly wouldn't let any distance come between us. I imagined her as the Robin to my Batman, the Tonto to my Lone Ranger. Her chubby little fingers had held mine during the entire drive to the *selo*.

Our coastline had always been fought over, understandably so. There was no place quite like it, so full of such impossible beauty. Dalmatia was the diamond of the Balkans and something that no other country had. One could travel the entire world and find no replacement for the waters of the Adriatic. Because of this, Dalmatia had always attracted people, and no one profited more from this than the Dalmatians. Surrounded by innumerable islands and endless blue water, the waves of tourists in the summertime became as expected as the sunrise each morning. We received visitors from all over, but it was the Western Europeans who took advantage of our nation's affordability more than anyone.

Most people allowed visitors to stay in their home for a small price, although taxes were quickly administered on those who accepted boarders. If one did not report the tourists staying at their residence, then they would incur a fine. However, being Eastern Europeans, we often found ways around this. Rules served more as 'guidelines', which not everyone chose to adhere to. Many people tried to pass off tourists as friends who were visiting (although this became hard to do once an individual had dozens of friends visiting simultaneously). Nonetheless, it wasn't as closely monitored in the villages as it was in the cities. That is why every year, up north in the *selo* that became my home away from home, there would always be one hundred or so German 'friends' visiting during the summer.

Summer in Dalmatia meant that an almost contagious sort of happiness seized the people. It was a time of relaxation, of socialising, of drinking and eating and swimming. The *selo* changed from a sleepy coastal dwelling into a bustling seaside escape—a place where comrades came to meet from all over the Balkans. Summer was the time of year when students would go back home or to the villages of their parents, away from the city life and from books and tests and cold mornings in small apartments.

Being in the *selo* also meant a suspension of every-day rules. I took advantage of our neighbours' generosity to the point of it being almost criminal.

Our closest neighbour was a man in his mid-sixties who we called Neno. Neno was retired and had, like my great uncle, chosen to dedicate himself to the village life. Every summer Neno's son, Dino, and his young family would come from Germany to spend their holidays in the *selo*. Dino was a *gastarbajter*, he worked as a low-level truck driver in Germany, but when he came back home, he was a king. He would arrive with his wife and two sons—who were slightly older than me—driving his silver Mercedes with the windows rolled down so that everyone could hear his trashy folk music blaring through the car's speakers.

There was nothing better than welcoming back the diaspora. For with the diaspora, came the gifts.

I was a good suck-up to 'Uncle Dino'. No matter how often my mother forbade me from asking for *anything*, even so much as a glass of water, I used my cunning to gain what I wanted. At Neno's house, when his son and family were in town, it was a cause for celebration. No child could ignore the blocks of German chocolate sitting on the kitchen counter, the fancy European sweets and drinks, the expensive-looking toys brought along by Dino's sons who quickly grew bored of their possessions. But I did not allow myself to get greedy—I had to be smart.

'Mama, I'm thirsty,' I would say, just loud enough to be heard, but still gentle enough not to appear as though I was complaining. My mother would shoot me a disapproving look, knowing exactly what I was doing.

'*Ajme*, let me get you something to drink you poor thing,' Dino's wife would proclaim. As planned, she went straight for a glass of ice-cold *Cockta*, a fizzy drink I only ever savoured during birthdays or for the New Year. I cherished each drop of that delicious dark liquid. Success.

'Thank you, *teta Jovana*,' I would reply in a disgustingly sweet and innocent voice I only ever used for such occasions.

'Jovana, give the girl some of that chocolate we brought! We have enough to feed the whole village,' Dino called out to his wife.

I smiled, feigning modesty and shyness.

'Such a good girl, how can I resist! Oh, to have a daughter like that, I would buy her chocolate for every day of the year,' Dino laughed, ruffling my hair.

I avoided my mother's irritated face while my father looked at me and shook his head, giving me a wink. Later, when no one could hear, Tata said to me, 'Mara, take everything they offer you! Don't be polite, these people are far from poor. Only a fool turns down a free meal.'

I obeyed without any reservations.

Autumn bled into winter sooner than one would have hoped. Winter lingered longer than necessary, so when the leaves finally began to return in spring, so did the smiles on people's faces.

During that time, I had grown a whole four centimetres. Things were looking positive. Then, on the day of my ninth birthday, our nation's President died. He was but days away from his eighty-eighth birthday, on which there would have been an annual country-wide celebration and the passing of the torch. Instead, a state of mourning began.

I was bitterly disappointed by this turn of events as it resulted in a severe lack of attention towards me or my birthday. I thought it very unfair that I had to compete with the popularity of the late President Tito, for there was no way I could get as many people to my birthday party as our *Predsednik* had at his funeral. In the end, I had to make do without a party, but I did receive a lovely surprise from Marko.

He called for me to come and join him in the courtyard, which he did by yelling my name towards my open window. I slipped on my shoes when I heard him and ran downstairs immediately. It was cool and breezy outside, but Marko was dressed in a singlet and shorts.

'Here, I got you this for your birthday,' he said to me after I joined him. 'My mum said I should get you a present, and I know you like to read, so ...'

I unwrapped the gift he gave me to reveal a beautiful copy of *The Little Prince*. My eyes lit up.

'Wow, Marko, this is perfect,' I said to him. He blushed a little and muttered what sounded like, 'You're welcome', before dragging me off to kick a soccer ball with him. I was so enraptured by the book that I began to read it immediately that night—after it had gotten too dark and all the neighbourhood kids had to disperse. For a short while, I was able to forget about President Tito and disappear into the different worlds of *Le Petit Prince*. I read aloud as Alisa drifted off to sleep and made it all the way to the part where the prince meets the fox. I soon succumbed to my heavy eyelids, vaguely absorbing the fox's important lesson: that what the heart can see was true, and often blind to the eye.

In response to our nation's tragedy, our school teacher assigned us each the task of writing a poem celebrating our lost leader. The best ones were chosen to be read out loud in front of everyone during a school assembly. A special ceremony was held in the school hall and we stood around waiting, as all the teachers held back tears.

I remember standing next to Ana, who, like me, was so taken aback by the faltering emotions of the adults that she dared not misbehave. We wore our *Pioneer* uniforms, the same hat and scarf that were given to us less than two years earlier. My white shirt and navy-blue skirt had been replaced every year in accordance to the extra centimetres that added to my height. Mama had very carefully arranged my hat onto my head that morning and wrapped the red scarf around my neck.

Nikola had been chosen to deliver a speech he had written himself; a perfectly understandable choice, seeing as he was without a doubt the brightest boy in our grade. I had written my own speech for the occasion, but my teacher had told me it was *too* honest. Apparently, I 'need not have gone into such detail explaining our President's protruding stomach and balding head', despite how distinguished I thought it made him look. I had focused too much on the man, quite literally, rather than on his achievements. It was a flaw I sought to correct in any future speeches I might write about dead presidents.

Nonetheless, my effort had been greater than Marko's, who, in his infinite wisdom, had decided simply to draw a visual representation of the President lying 'peacefully' in his coffin, not withholding signs of bodily decay and worm infestations. I quite liked it and appreciated the artistic talent that Marko had demonstrated; our teacher, however, disagreed. Marko had to endure a meeting with the principal for that act of self-expression and even his parents were informed. It was after this particular incident that Marko had been singled-out as a 'potential troublemaker'.

Marko knew this, too, and I could tell that it hurt him to be labelled so quickly, despite his cavalier attitude. I sometimes felt as though he genuinely did not understand why his actions caused controversy on occasion. The Marko I had gotten to know was certainly cheeky, but he was also inherently good and thoughtful. Whilst listening to Nikola read out his speech, I looked down at the line of students assembled in a neat row until I saw Marko, who gave me a quick grin. He managed to lift my spirits in spite of the funeral-like tone of the school's assembly hall. I looked at him and saw nothing but a boy with smiling eyes, whose face was kind.

'Everything will go to hell now, just you watch,' Baka Roza said.

My mother shot her a disapproving look, but Baka did not take notice. She was watching the small television in the kitchen whilst peeling potatoes, helping to make a side dish for Mama's stuffed capsicums. The smell of boiling vegetables filled the air. Whilst the adults commented on politics, all I could think about was how hungry I was.

'Don't be so negative, Mama,' my father said from the comfort of the sofa. He was rolling up some tobacco into a cigarette, sweating from the concentration it required. He had an open bottle of beer on the table in front of him, which he was careful not to knock over each time he reached for some more tobacco. I found myself staring at the stains on the old singlet he was wearing, which I presumed at some point must have been white but was now a faded grey colour.

'Oh, don't be so naïve, Lazar,' Baka Roza responded. 'When has anything ever gone right for us in this country? You will see—all the crazies will come out now.'

The combined smell of roasted capsicum, beer and tobacco, partnered with my family's political commentary, was starting to make me feel sick and claustrophobic. I went out onto the balcony for some air despite the irritating heat that swept over me.

As I was looking down below, I saw a familiar figure: Marko, walking in the direction of the corner shop. I was about to call out to him but stopped myself once I saw his father follow him. He looked as though he was telling Marko off, raising his voice at him and gesturing violently. Suddenly he delivered a swift slap to the back of Marko's head. It shocked me to see how far Marko's body lurched forwards after being hit.

I could not make out what Marko's father was saying as he stormed into the corner shop with Marko at his footsteps. I remained on the balcony, waiting for the father and son to exit. Marko's father still had a menacing look on his face, but he was no longer paying as much attention to his son. I suppose Marko was grateful for that. I saw Marko exit the shop a moment later, carrying a crate of beer.

Marko looked up in the direction of my balcony. We made eye contact, and I smiled at him as best I could. Did he know I had witnessed the entire scene? Marko looked away as though he felt ashamed. I thought to myself that I must make a point of mentioning to my friend that my father also drank beer and could get mad sometimes. Really, our fathers were probably quite similar ... except, of course, that my father nursed my bruises, rather than created them.

Chapter 5

Once, when I asked Mama why she had chosen to marry Tata despite all the other men in the world, she told me it was because he was *different*. When I asked how he was *different*, she answered by saying, 'He drank his tea with milk in it, while everyone else drank theirs without it or only did if they were sick.'

I later learned this meant that Tata had his own way of doing things. He refused to limit himself to his surroundings, *or* to his choice of tea, straying from the herbal classics of chamomile and rose-hip and preferring something a little more *hard-hitting*. He had spent months courting my mother, attempting to impress her and win her over, but it was not until one particular date during an autumn afternoon, when they stopped in a cafe for a hot drink together, and he had ordered his black tea with milk, that my mother realised her feelings for him. From that moment onwards they remained together.

Tata took Mama and me out dancing on the eve of my tenth birthday to celebrate my reaching double digits. I was excited to spend the evening doing something as mature and as elegant as *dancing*. Mama had her crimson lipstick and her lilac dress on. She saw me watching her do her make-up, and her reflection in the mirror smiled back at me.

The night, now as I remember it, was perfectly warm and enticing, as though the night itself could not wait for summer and for the rush of people that came with it. We strolled to the local hall, my parents hand in hand while I jubilantly led the way. From the outside, music could be heard, and the sound of muffled footsteps and booming laughter interrupted the melody every so often. I was feeling far more grown-up than my age.

My father made quite an impact upon entering a room, since his presence alone was so commanding it could not help but attract the eyes of others. In this particular instance, I think he was glad for the attention, since he swelled with pride and took both mine and my mother's hand as he walked into the hall. He embodied success, and it was infectious.

Later on, and with the benefit of hindsight, I came to realise that my perception of my father was largely my own; blown-up and glorified, faultless and idyllic. Many of my beliefs concerning my father were certainly not untrue; he was indeed successful and loved by many. But my love was unconditional, and I did not understand how love could have any conditions attached to it at all.

Nonetheless, I was still young enough to believe that the sight of my Mama and Tata dancing away like two teenagers newly in love was the absolute norm; that *all* parents felt the same way about each other and that *all* parents stayed together and that *all* parents loved their children so much so that they would gladly take them out dancing for an evening even if it meant staying up past their bed-time. Why should it be any different for anyone else?

On that very night as my father picked me up and lifted me high, placed my own two feet on top of his own and proceeded to waltz me across the dance floor, my mother looked on and smiled, regretfully unaware that merely minutes away in a small apartment, her only sister was being beaten by the man she had vowed to spend her life with. With each graceful dance my mother had partaken in with the one she loved, her sister had been hit just as many times by her husband, with a ferocity and bitterness she was told was as strong as his love for her—a love so strong that it could not be controlled and simply *had* to be expressed in such a way.

That night I was carried home by Tata, exhausted in his arms, and was tucked into bed by Mama, who still did not see me as 'too old' to be tucked in, despite my milestone in age. Across town my auntie did not cry herself to sleep, but instead stayed silent in fear of waking her slumbering husband.

The summer had passed by with great tension. There was action, there was emotion, there was everything needed to make for a fantastic Spanish soap-opera—the kind that Baka Roza genuinely adored and took up most of her weekday afternoons with.

After not having seen her for quite some time, Aunt Dragana turned up at our door one day in early June—her excuses having ranged from 'I have an appointment' to 'I haven't been well' and even 'The carpet needs cleaning, sorry'. This time it was 'He's beaten me, again,' whilst attempting to cover her bruises with a balaclava and heavy clothing in such warm weather.

All my mother could summon was the feeble sentence, 'What do you mean, *again?*' before her big sister burst into tears and let herself in. I shuffled towards my bedroom, not yet sure whether this was one of those moments where the adults needed their privacy. In those moments, I'd pretend to walk away but instead I hid behind the door and eavesdropped.

For a moment, I did not even recognise my aunt behind her absurd outfit. I thought she had joined the local crazy of the town, who was known for wearing heavy winter clothing in the summer months. But then she took off the balaclava and the sweater, and I saw more black and blue patches than actual skin.

Without any due warning, my father stood up from the dining chair where he was nursing his Turkish coffee, stormed out of the room and straight out of the front door.

'Oh, God,' was all I heard my mother say. She ran after him, yelling his name, telling her sister not to dare follow them. As I did my best to act the wallflower in this whole scenario, Alisa tottered out of our bedroom in a very blasé fashion, and straight into the arms of Aunt Dragana. It was good timing, too, for it seemed to give my aunt a welcome distraction and even provoked a hint of a smile across her face.

Aunt Dragana kept us 'entertained' while my parents were mysteriously absent. I attempted to understand the magnitude of the situation, but felt terrified at the thought of saying something inappropriate, so I opted to say nothing at all. I was grateful for my sister who did all the talking for us, but I squirmed in my seat at the uncomfortable feeling that arose as she began to ask questions typical of her age, demanding to know why, why, *why*. She had to ask *why* auntie looked funny, *why* her skin was spotted, *why* does that happen.

I couldn't help but laugh a little when Aunt Dragana managed to sell Alisa a story of how auntie had been climbing trees and was not careful and fell out of a tree and managed to hit every branch on the way down. I pictured the thought of Mama's big sister like a giant, awkward monkey, swinging from branch to branch until losing her grip and falling in a comical way. I smiled at the thought, but it immediately evaporated when I reminded myself that, unfortunately, it was not the truth.

My parents returned about three quarters of an hour later, to find my aunt, Alisa and myself plonked on the couch and watching cartoons. The look on my mother's face was one I had never seen before— like a deer that had just narrowly escaped the bonnet of a pick-up truck—whereas my father's entire appearance was absolutely fear-inducing. He looked as though he had just killed a man, and for a moment I thought he might have. And I had a feeling I knew exactly which man.

'I sorted him out,' was all Tata said. He then walked to the cabinet and poured a shot of *rakija* from the glass decanter, his hand shaking. He downed the shot in one stroke and proceeded to pour another.

I took Alisa from the room and into our bedroom feeling it was the proper thing to do, whilst growing weary of her attempts at maintaining my undivided attention. I was trying to overhear the grownups' conversation, after all. I sat as close as possible to the entrance of the living room and attempted to hear what was going on.

From what I gathered, my uncle Jovan had received his 'comeuppance' and that was that. I was not sure what 'comeuppance' was or what it meant, but it sounded bad. Either way, apparently it was now safe for Aunt Dragana to go back home, since, to quote dear Tata, 'That monster wouldn't dare try to pull that crap again.'

It was but two weeks after the 'comeuppance' incident that Aunt Dragana announced to us that she and her family were moving to Belgrade. My mother was devastated at the news, but more than anything she was worried.

'Jovan has been offered a new job,' Dragana told us.

'What? Where?' my father asked. 'He's a plumber! There's thousands of them!'

'I don't know, he didn't say ...' my aunt trailed off. The conversation did not progress much further, like those little metal balls that go back and forth knocking into each other until all energy is exhausted and they become perfectly still. My parents seemed to know that this was an excuse, that we were losing Dragana to her husband once more, that he was removing her from safety and taking the family to the concrete landscape that is *New Belgrade*.

'Nenad will get to go to university there. It will be great. There will be more opportunities there.' Aunt Dragana sounded as though she was trying to convince herself more than anyone else.

'What about Nataša?' asked my mother, referring to Nenad's older sister.

'She will stay in Zagreb,' said Dragana. 'And anyway, she is so busy with exams and looking for an internship ...'

Throughout the discussion I looked at my mother, who appeared as though she was watching her family disappear before her eyes. Her younger brother, Branislav, was already living in Sarajevo with his wife, Selma. He and my mother were close, but we rarely got to see them. Now Mama was going to lose her sister too, and Belgrade was even further away than Sarajevo. Not only that, but Baka and Dida would get even fewer visitors in Lika from now on. I saw her mind at work, thinking about all the implications, and most of all, just how sad it would make her.

After Aunt Dragana left our apartment, I observed my parents and their concerned expressions. They could not understand why Dragana would go back to Jovan at all, let alone agree to move to another city. As my mother began to get more visibly upset, Tata attempted to comfort her.

'It's going to be alright,' he told her. 'Yes, they are moving away, but it's not the end of the world, right? I mean, it's not as though we won't be able to see them, right? Everything will be the same as always, you'll see. I mean, it's not as though they're moving to a different country. It's not as though they're no longer in Yugoslavia.'

Chapter 6

We should have known it wouldn't last long, but, in all honesty, everyone had given up on Aunt Dragana finding the strength to get away. We underestimated her.

Aunt Dragana called Mama one evening to announce that she was divorcing Jovan. After almost a year with no signs of improvement and several visits from the local police, Jovan was forced to move out of their apartment in New Belgrade. He did not resist, but instead made a point of saying to his soon-to-be ex-wife that no one, not even his children, would ever hear from him again. Aunt Dragana thought this to be a blessing.

Aunt Dragana was relieved but struggling; despite everything working out for the better, there was still an absence in her life. She was without a husband. Had it not been for Nenad, her pain would have consumed her. He handled his father's departure with maturity, immediately taking on the role of the man of the house. He notified his sister in Zagreb and she promised to come and visit Nenad and her mother the moment she could get away from university. My mother also promised to come and visit. The next weekend, after receiving news of the divorce, Alisa, Mama and I were boarding a train to Belgrade.

I loved Belgrade from the moment I set foot in the city.

The metropolis was nothing like the home I was used to; it could not be seen and experienced in thirty minutes of gentle strolling. It was buzzing, thriving and purely *alive*. The people looked different, more individual and interesting. I did not know where to look first. But what I loved most was being able to see my cousins.

'Back in 1979 I went and watched the rock band, *Azra*, play at the *Lapidarij Club* in Zagreb for the first time,' my cousin, Nenad, told me. He was regaling me with tales of his youth and he seemed to be in a perpetual state of movement and activity. He continued speaking whilst he gently removed a vinyl record from its sleeve and placed it onto the record player.

'It was a small dark place set out in a sort of L-shape,' he continued. 'The best time to be there was probably around September, when all the bars and theatres began to reopen for the students coming back to study. A photo taken of the band performing became the cover of their first album. *Marco Polo* was the café to hang out in. I don't know what it's like now, but I hope one day you'll get to go there.'

He was speaking at what seemed to be a million miles a second about things I had not heard of. Rock bands, clubs and bars, student protests and art and theatre and literature. It all felt so *romantic* and I couldn't help but want to be a part of it.

Once Nataša had arrived from Zagreb, she and Nenad did their best to be my tour guides and educators. Nenad, for someone who had only been living in Belgrade for a relatively short time, appeared to know every nook and cranny of the city and all it had to offer. He walked me through *Skadarlija*, the artists' corner and around every passage of the *Kalemegdan* fortress. He spoke of where all the good bands played, where the best spots were to run into famous actors and which bars were the best for drinking in.

'That's some great advice to give to an eleven-year-old, Nenad,' his sister would say to him sarcastically.

Nenad would look at me and wink and argue that quite often the most useful information cannot be learned at school.

I had memorised the bus route from New Belgrade to the city centre. I had learned the name of every person and place my cousins mentioned to me. I was thoroughly enjoying all the city had to offer. Our presence in Belgrade also had a calming effect on my aunt and my cousins.

The same could not really be said for the arrival of my mother's uncle.

Great Uncle Miki was Baka Anka's younger brother—a typical farmer, full of brawn and good advice about cheese. He was a widow and had but one son, and therefore he viewed his two nieces as though they were his own two daughters. His son, Tomo, was also close with his cousins, in particular with my uncle Branislav. Tomo had an intellectual disability, and, as mild as it was, it had left him largely socially isolated. He had left high school as soon as he could in order to work on the farm with his father, which he did with utmost perfection.

All the docility and tenderness in the world appeared to have been bestowed upon my Baka Anka, meaning there was not much left of it for her younger brother. Miki was forthright, thuggish and always to the point, but tactful enough to know what *not* to say. At least most of the time, anyway. I loved him though, for he always knew how to shake things up.

'Ubiću ga!' *I'll kill him*, was the first proclamation he made upon walking into Aunt Dragana's apartment. *Here we go*, I had thought, *some action already*. My mother and her sister said nothing, knowing perfectly well that no discussion could ensue until Uncle Miki had had his necessary half hour of enraged rambling.

The Turkish coffee was already brewing. Aunt Dragana was using her largest *džezva*, which meant business. Uncle Miki greeted his two nieces, kissing each on the cheek three times, the Serbian way, hugging them both tightly and all the while growing more engrossed in his rant. He paused only to greet us children, grabbing Nenad and Nataša in a rough embrace, the two of them looking as though they had hoped to have outgrown this hugging business. Fortunately, Alisa and I were hugged with a little more gentleness and Uncle Miki presented us each with a block of chocolate. I smiled and shot a glance at Nenad, who looked disappointed to have apparently outgrown this business of being given chocolate.

'You can share with me,' I said to him, and he laughed.

'Thanks, Mara. I would've stolen some from you anyway,' Nenad replied. He came and sat between Alisa and me, while Nataša remained on the couch opposite us, pretending to read whilst really keeping her ears open for any interesting piece of conversation.

Dexys Midnight Runners were playing on the TV as Uncle Miki lit up a cigarette and stared at the screen, not really looking at the band or listening to their music. He exhaled a large cloud of smoke from his mouth, which wafted across the screen and momentarily blurred the men in their overalls. 'What is this? Who are these princesses?' Miki muttered under his breath, shaking his head. 'You know what the problem is? It's men like this!' I saw Nataša lift her head slightly, in order to roll her eyes. She shot a condescending look at Miki.

'They don't make men like they used to,' Uncle Miki carried on. 'None of them know what it means to do a proper day's hard work. They're all a bunch of *pičkice*, if you ask me. Sorry, kids.'

I tried not to laugh at Uncle Miki's comparison between modern men and female genitalia. My mother waved her hand back and forth in the air in Alisa and my direction, as though it would shoo the dirty word away and out of our memories. Too late. I couldn't help but smile to myself, looking at my giant great uncle in his old and faded blue-collar shirt, a cigarette in one hand and a *tiny* coffee cup in the other, decorated with ornamental flowers.

'Dragana, there is no excuse for what that animal did to you. But I never did like the look of him. You know what he—'

'I know, Miki, please, let's change the subject,' Dragana interrupted.

'Change the subject?! What, and act like nothing happened? Let him carry on with his life? *Ma!*'

'We all know what happened, Miki,' my mother said. 'There's not much more to say. Everyone is better off now.'

'Dragana, that man was no good. He was neither here nor there. Obviously, he was no intellectual, but at least he could have made up for that somehow. He should have become an army man, like Lazar, that would have sorted him out. He would've thought twice about laying a hand on anyone after feeling what it's like to follow orders.'

I could feel Nenad fidgeting next to me uncomfortably. I had never experienced what he was experiencing now. To have to sit and listen to constant criticisms about your own father, about someone who contributed to half of who you are. I never felt ashamed of who my father was and is; if anything, I felt proud. But we are not our fathers. For all the bad ex-uncle Jovan had, Nenad and Nataša were filled with an equivalent amount of goodness.

The awkwardness subsided and the conversation turned to other things, like the future and our family. Nataša had begun to read her book for real and Nenad had helped devour my entire block of chocolate with me. He then turned his attention to Alisa, who was far too young and small to finish an entire meal of anything.

'Too much sugar is not good for little kids,' Nenad said to my sister as he took the block of chocolate from her. 'You clearly need my help, Alisa.'

Uncle Miki hung around for the whole day and made himself useful come lunch time. He was an amazing cook, the product of a lifetime spent on the farm. I thought I was too full to eat, after an afternoon spent snacking on sweets, but the smell of beans and speck with fresh bread quickly revived my appetite. We spent the afternoon eating and drinking, enjoying each other's company in the warm summer heat. Eventually Uncle Miki had to leave and head back home. He made us all promise to come and visit him some time and maybe 'learn a thing or two' at the farm. I thought this sounded exciting, but my older cousins exchanged looks of uncertainty, indicating that previous experience had taught them otherwise.

We said goodbye to Uncle Miki, and Aunt Dragana walked him out to his car as the sun finally started to lose its sting. The concrete block landscape of New Belgrade looked like grey dominoes in front of an orange-purple backdrop, the large expanses of asphalt trapping all the heat at ground level. I lingered downstairs a bit longer, whilst rush hour heralded waves of people returning home. As the sun set, the shadows elongated, so that teenage girls would cast longing glances at their falsely lengthened limbs, and children would perform leap-frog jumps in vain attempts to capture their own elusive Peter Pan. This was *Novi Beograd*.

It was quite difficult when the time came for us to leave Belgrade. Aunt Dragana looked sad, but she assured us she was better; better than she had been, at any rate. I suggested she spend some time going out with her son, since he seemed to know how to have a good time. She laughed at this and said she would leave that to me, for when I was a little older.

Chapter 7

The winter of '83 was one I spent largely indoors, listening to The Clash's album, *Combat Rock*, a gift from Nenad. I had welcomed in the New Year to the sound of 'Rock the Casbah' and spent the money I was given over the holiday on purchasing all four previous albums The Clash had released. It was money well spent. And as much as I loved my cousin's gift, my favourite album by far was *London Calling*.

Evidently, I had entered my punk-rock phase.

At first, Marko acted as though my newfound interest in this brilliant style of music was pathetic. But after a few weeks of not being able to stop singing the words *should I stay or should I go*, (the only words I think he knew in English), Marko was converted.

'Ok, maybe it's not that bad,' he confessed to me during one spring afternoon. We were sitting on the swings in the park, which was full of other children, preparing ourselves for the warmer weather.

'Not bad?' I said. 'It's amazing! I wish I could go to England ...'

'We've got everything we need right here,' Marko said, indicating with a sweeping motion of his arm the scene before us. 'And anyway, who says we don't have musicians?'

He was right. Marko was growing quite proficient in his

knowledge of music. Whether it was an attempt to outdo me or something out of genuine interest, he had managed to accumulate an impressive record collection within a matter of weeks. I attributed this to him being an only child; nothing was difficult for Marko to obtain.

'Which reminds me,' he went on, 'I got a new record. Let's go listen to it.'

We strolled back to Marko's apartment, never straying from the topic of music. I had to admit that Marko was the best of the best when it came to the subject. Ana had excellent taste as well, but she tended to sometimes wander off into the pop arena, preferring the likes of *Magazin, Zana* and later on the more tolerable, *Đavoli*. Nikola was incredibly knowledgeable, but too experimental for my liking, often citing bands I hadn't even heard of. He was always ahead of the times, it seemed.

We got to Marko's place and were greeted by his mother, who I knew loved me more than I deserved. I was always polite and respectful, but I was not sure what I had done to earn her attention and interest. I relished it, nonetheless, especially as it irritated Marko. His mother brought out snacks, which she appeared to have a self-replenishing supply of in her kitchen cupboard.

'How are your parents, Mara? How is school? Tell your mother I said *hello!*'

I barely ever had time for a reply, so I smiled and nodded as I stuffed *Smoki* into my mouth, getting my fingers greasy and shiny.

'*Krivo Srastanje*,' Marko said to me, holding the record as though it were some sacred item. He placed it with poise onto the record player and set the needle with the grace and precision of a brain surgeon performing a life-saving operation on the President. The record began to turn, and the tune to '*3N*' started. It was the first of about five thousand times that I was to listen to that song; the only song that was capable of turning my attention away from The Clash and all thoughts of England.

'All you kids seem to be doing these days is listening to music!' Marko's mother called from the other room.

Marko smiled at me and said, 'It's all that's worth doing.'

We may not have understood the lyrics perfectly at that age, we may not have picked up on the subtleties and nuances, but we loved the sound more than anything we had heard before. *Azra* was being played all around us, by our friends, by the older high schoolers, by the university students who were feeling disillusioned and disenfranchised. It became the voice of a generation, of people of various ages and experiences, all of us the inhabitants of a land that was not going to last much longer, but that had raised us and made us who we were.

It had been organised as an end of year school trip that our class was to go on a three-day trip to Titograd, the capital of Montenegro. Most of us had never travelled to this part of the country and were naturally excited beyond all reason, as though we were being flown to the sandy beaches of Hawaii. Living by the coast, many of us rarely ventured elsewhere during the summertime, for it seemed so illogical.

We were experiencing beautiful springtime weather on the day of our departure, which made for an even more exhilarating experience. Children and their parents began turning up early that Saturday morning, knowing that the bus was set to leave by 8a.m. sharp. The time had been drilled into our heads repeatedly, and it was no surprise everyone had endeavoured to turn up even earlier than needed.

Everyone, of course, except for Marko.

I had arrived at school where the coach bus was waiting and had proceeded to help my father load my small luggage bag into the bus. Nikola was there, of course, with his mother, and Ana was already saying her goodbyes to her parents. Most of my classmates were already on board the bus and securing themselves a good window seat, or one in the back row, which was always the first to be taken. But I kept looking around, starting to get worried at Marko's noticeable absence.

'Don't worry, Mara,' my mother said to me. 'He will turn up, or I'm sure there's a reasonable explanation for it. Just go and enjoy yourself.'

I nodded and took the bag she was waving before me. As always, it was packed full of food, enough for what seemed like the entirety of my time away. I know she had only meant it for the duration of the bus ride, though.

Ana was calling me to hurry up, so I hugged my parents. Mama plastered me with kisses and Tata hugged me hard enough to lift me off the ground. I bent down to hug Alisa and I told her I would miss her. It was true; I *would* miss her. This was the first time since she was born that I'd be away from her. I made my parents promise to read to her before bedtime, as I had done every night.

I made my way onto the bus then, where there was still no sign of Marko, and I took my place next to Ana, who had reserved a seat for me.

'Where is he?' I asked her, not needing to explain whom I was referring to.

'Oh, who knows. I'm not even surprised. Marko runs on his own time,' she replied. A moment later the bus started up and all the students began to cheer, as we slowly took off towards our destination. I looked behind me and caught Nikola's gaze, and he returned a confused expression and shrugged his shoulders, mouthing the words 'I have no idea.' I turned back towards the front and tuned in to Ana, who had begun to recite everything she wanted to see and do in Titograd. I didn't want to disappoint her by pointing out we were most likely going to get dragged along to educational locations, to be lectured about our nation's greatness, and that this was not a shopping trip. Instead, I listened as she listed the different things she planned to buy.

It took us over eight hours to arrive in Titograd, including all the stops and toilet breaks on the way. By this time, the 'thrill' of the bus ride had worn off long before (it had only taken a couple of hours) and we were all more than happy to have our feet meet the ground.

The bus had brought us to our modest hotel in the city. Evening was soon to set in and tonight was going to be a night for eating and resting, before we set off to see the sights the following day.

The air was still warm and I had enough strength in me to feel some sense of anticipation and joy at being in a new place. But then I remembered who was missing. And just as my thoughts were about to turn to the whereabouts of Marko, he appeared before me. Literally. He appeared before all of us, strolling out of the hotel entrance, smiling.

'Marko?' I called out. At the sound of my voice everyone turned to where I was looking, and the class erupted into cheers once more at the sight of Marko. Our teacher stood in disbelief, shaking her head, her mouth wide open and her chins wobbling in shock.

'Mr Ivanić,' she managed to say to Marko, her voice now as stern as ever. 'Does a phone call to your parents need to be made, by any chance?'

Marko looked at her. 'Yes, Mrs Danilović. They probably want to know where I am.'

She looked at him with a disapproving eye before finally offering a hint of a grin at Marko's aptitude for scheming. Mrs Danilović called us all to come inside and prepare for dinner while she made an 'important phone call' from reception.

In the hotel, I finally said, 'Well? Explain yourself!'

'Just a common misunderstanding,' Marko said. 'I thought the bus left at 9a.m., not 8a.m., so I was a bit late.' He laughed at this and then I asked him what had happened.

'My dad was pissed off, obviously,' Marko said with a slight sting in his voice. 'He said I was an unreliable idiot and I didn't

55

deserve to go anywhere. He left me there with my backpack and told me to walk back home.' I looked downwards, feeling my stomach clench at the harshness of those words. But Marko continued on, undeterred.

'Well, clearly I wasn't going to miss the class trip!' he said. 'I figured, how hard can it be to get to Titograd? Just follow the coastline, right? So I walked back towards the main road and decided to hitch a ride. I had to wait twenty minutes before a truck driver stopped. He was on his way to Šibenik, so I said "perfect" and hopped in.'

Nikola and Ana were standing by my side, with the whole class now crowding around us. Everyone wanted to know how Marko had managed to turn up to Titograd, and before any of us.

'Well, I got off at Šibenik,' Marko continued. 'There, the truck driver helped me find another truck driver and explained my situation. The next guy was great. He took me as far as Dubrovnik, all the way past Split. He even bought me food on the way. And two ice-creams! Then when we got to Dubrovnik, he called a friend who is a taxi driver. He made a deal with his friend to get me safely to Titograd and he would make it up to him. The guy said, "No problem", and he drove me straight here. We were having such a good time chatting that I think he could have kept driving past Titograd and all the way through to Bulgaria.'

We all laughed at Marko's story and were glad to have him here. Nikola marvelled at how, even when Marko was late, he still had to be the first to get here—always the show-off. Marko laughed and put Nikola in a headlock, until our teacher turned up and told us all off for being a nuisance.

I was relieved to see Marko had arrived safely in Titograd, but not shocked. For some reason, none of us were particularly scared by what he had done. It didn't occur to us that something could have gone wrong. Even Marko's parents weren't angry, they were just glad he had the sense to tell them where he was. Marko's father was even proud for a brief moment, impressed by his son's adaptability.

When we had a moment to ourselves in Titograd, Marko took me aside and handed me something.

'Here, I picked this up on one of my stop-overs to Titograd,' he said. I took it from his hands and saw that it was a book. *The Hobbit*. I looked at Marko, dumbfounded by his thoughtfulness.

'Did you steal this?' I asked.

'Of course not!' he replied defensively. 'I bought the book with my own money, believe it or not. I know you read his other books, what were they called, *King of the Rings* or something.'

'*Lord of the Rings*.'

'Yeah, it's not important. Anyway, I thought I would get bored from all the driving and I might even read it myself. Don't know what I was thinking. It's yours to keep.'

'Thanks, Marko,' I said to him. He smiled at me and shrugged it off. I briefly wondered to myself what else Marko had managed to do whilst travelling to Titograd. He was so predictable yet so surprising at the same time. But nothing was difficult for him. Marko always found a way to get through life without overthinking things, especially consequences. Fortunately for him, things often seemed to go his way and he would come out on top, unharmed.

Maybe Marko had just been lucky, or maybe that had all occurred during a time when *brotherhood and unity* still existed. Marko had no worries about asking anyone for help or about hitching a ride with some strangers halfway across the country's coastline. And no one had hesitated to help a young student arrive safely to the class excursion he didn't want to miss.

Nonetheless, we all took extra care on the way back to make sure that everyone was accounted for and that Marko, in particular, was the first to board the bus. Marko scoffed at the measures Mrs Danilović took in making sure he was not to go missing in action.

'I don't doubt you'd have any issues in getting back to Zadar yourself, Mr Ivanić, but I'd rather not have you disrupting any more innocent travellers,' she said to him. Marko pulled an expression as though to say 'fair enough' and secured himself a window seat on the bus.

I took a seat next to him and proceeded to read my new book.

'Marko, you will be late to your own funeral one day,' I said to him without looking up. He laughed a little and leaned back in his seat, closing his eyes.

'That's alright,' he said. 'Just promise me they'll play some good music to see me off, okay, Mara?'

'I wouldn't have it any other way, Marko.'

Chapter 8

The basketball hit me hard on the head, messing up my ponytail in the process.

'*Hahaha!*' Marko laughed like a madman, as I turned to swear at him. 'You're going to have to improve your reflexes if you want to even *consider* playing basketball with me,' Marko said.

'Reflexes, I have. It's eyes in the back of my head that I'm missing,' I replied. I was growing tired of Marko's teaching tactics. He insisted on the approach of throwing basketballs at me while I wasn't looking, believing it helped 'build my peripheral vision'. I, however, was equally insistent that he did not know the meaning of the word 'peripheral', and that he perhaps lacked the skills required to coach someone in basketball.

'Ok,' he said, starting to take pity on me. 'Let's call it a day. I think you need a break. We can go play with dolls or something for a while, do whatever it is that you girls do.' I looked at him and shook my head, fully aware of his attempt to get me wound up.

'I'm sorry, all my dolls are still at your place from the last time you borrowed them,' I said to him. Marko feigned to throw the ball at me again, as I dodged out of his way. We teased each other in the same roundabout way until we reached our courtyard.

'Are you going to Lika this summer?' Marko asked me.

'Yeah, for a week or so, to see my grandparents. Then it's off to the *selo*,' I replied.

Marko nodded, thinking this over. We were standing in the courtyard of our apartment blocks, passing the basketball back and forth to each other.

Where I often made trips to Lika and the *selo* up north, Marko had family across from town, on the island, *Pašman*. That was where his grandparents lived and where he was obliged to spend most of his summer. He enjoyed it, but I knew he was sometimes envious of me, for I usually spent time with a whole new crowd in the *selo*, and of course Nikola had a place there too. All of Ana's family were in town and as she got older, her parents gave her permission to travel with friends up north. Marko surely felt slightly left out, but I kind of savoured time away from him. At least I could dedicate more attention to the others.

I chose to make my way to the *selo* with Nikola's family, since they usually spent more time there than my parents did. Nikola's father was the one who had a small house in the village, left to him by his father and grandfather before him. Like my family, Nikola's family had a long history of living in the villages beneath Velebit, and his ancestors had settled in Dalmatia further back than anyone could trace. Vesna drove the car there, with Aco in the front seat and Nikola and me in the back. We drove carefully because Nikola's father had been unwell recently and his body had weakened. But as per usual, he was in good spirits and looking forward to coming out of the apartment to inhale the salty mountain air.

In the back of the car, Nikola handed me a flat, rectangular package. It was wrapped in brown paper and tied with string.

'Don't open it yet, it's a present. Wait until we arrive,' he said.

'What did you get me a present for?' I exclaimed, completely surprised. I really hoped he hadn't spent any money on me.

'Don't worry, it didn't cost me anything,' Nikola said, as though he had read my thoughts. 'I'm sorry I couldn't give it to you earlier, for your birthday, but it wasn't quite … ready. You'll see what I mean.'

I was excited for the remainder of the trip and was feeling quite restless, struggling to stop myself from opening the gift. Nikola was particularly proud of himself for having made me wait so long before opening the package—a fun kind of torture for him.

When we arrived at the village, we could already see the tourists congregating, the cafes full of people and the sea littered with sailboats and rafts. I felt at home and at peace, so sure that I could never love any place as much as I loved this one. We made our way to Nikola's house, a small, stone structure. Its plain appearance was compensated by its prime location just metres away from the water's edge.

After quickly helping to unpack our belongings, I seized the present Nikola had given me. I made no effort to be gentle, shredding the wrapping paper apart to reveal the contents of the package.

I opened it to find the most amazing painting.

'My dad did it, of course. He said it's a special one for you,' Nikola said.

The painting was a scene of the sunset on the Adriatic, the same view that could be seen looking out from Nikola's small home in the *selo*. It was painted on a silk canvas, giving the picture a beautiful and mesmerising texture.

'Go, look out the front window when the sun sets and you'll see it's just like the picture,' Nikola explained. He was smiling at me, taking in my reaction.

'This is the best thing anyone has ever given to me,' I managed to say. I said thank you about a thousand times and gave Nikola a huge hug.

We admired the picture some more, and every time I looked at it, I noticed something new and more beautiful about it.

'I have to go and thank your dad, he didn't need to do this for me,' I said to Nikola.

'Yes, he did,' Nikola replied.

'No really, he didn't,' I said.

'No, Mara, he *did*. He had to do it now, otherwise he could never do it,' Nikola said more firmly.

I looked up at him about to ask what he meant, but the expression on his face told me. Nikola's smile had disappeared and was replaced by a sombre look I had never before seen on his face.

'What do you mean?' I asked, fearing the response.

'He's dying, Mara,' was all that my friend managed to say.

I stood there, speechless, feeling so unprepared for what I had just heard. I stopped myself from asking him what he meant, from asking whether he was sure. Aco was dying.

I reached out and took his hand, and then his other hand, slowly pulling Nikola into my arms. I felt his body give itself up as though it had wanted nothing more than to fall into an embrace. I was surprised at how light he was, almost like a child. I held him like that for a long time, until he let go and looked at me. He nodded at me, as though to signify he was all right now and we could carry on as usual.

I wondered how I would thank Aco for the painting without bursting into tears in front of him. When I saw him there, sitting on a chair beside his wife, looking out the window, I decided not to bother them. And I noticed Nikola was right. The view from the house was exactly like my painting.

I stayed at Nikola's place just for the night before moving into my own family's home. Great Uncle Dmitar was waiting for me and I felt I owed him some company. I also felt like Nikola needed the time alone with his father. It was all they had left together, and it wasn't mine to take up. Nikola still invited me over though, insisting that my presence was more than welcome. I tried my best to ignore the strained atmosphere, but I knew my face gave me away.

Our neighbour, Neno, was happy to see me too, and announced that his son would soon be arriving. No less than a day later, Dino the *gastarbajter* did indeed arrive with his wife, Jovana. His sons had outgrown family holidays, but it did not stop Dino from bringing months' worth of supplies and goods, which he gladly handed out to me. But no matter how much *Kinder* chocolate I ate, it could do nothing to distract me from the news Nikola had given me. Despite my overwhelming sadness, I spent every day with Nikola and his parents, just as he insisted; and somehow, his sorrow, and mine, became a little easier to bear.

The summer days passed by in a bittersweet slowness, as though easing us into the colder seasons and the inevitable sadness we knew would come with them. I spent many early mornings hiking across the rocky terrain of the *selo*, Nikola accompanying me and pointing out where to watch for snakes or spiders. He knew this land like no one else. He was the one who had spent his childhood acting as the man of the house, venturing outdoors whenever needed in order to help the neighbours herd their goats or collect the herbs that grew nearby. Alas, as with most cases where people gradually move to urbanised locations and away from their village roots, Nikola's family home in the *selo* had dilapidated considerably over time due to lack of maintenance. Nikola, as well, had grown out of certain practices that came with living in rustic conditions.

We spoke, almost out of a great necessity to do so, about life and death. But I found myself short for words when it came to such a topic, perhaps because I did not see myself as wise or knowledgeable enough to offer any useful or meaningful insight. Instead, I gave whatever words of comfort came to my mind and attempted to deliver them through the softness of my lips and voice. I spoke with Nikola in a way that I had never spoken to anyone before. I could not imagine having such a conversation with Marko, or even with Ana. But of course, they did not have to think about such terrible realities, fortunately.

I found it difficult to communicate any feelings of hope. My lack of faith meant that I never found solace in thoughts of everlasting life and loved ones 'meeting on the other side'. I just did not believe any of this to be true; when considering it all, looking at the big picture, I felt that we all have but this one life. Yet to say this to Nikola, who was facing the impending loss of his father, felt rude and insensitive. So I did not say much, for I did not want to lie.

I could tell from what Nikola was saying to me that he was not a strong believer, but desperately wanted to be one. He wanted to believe in it all and have that hope, and, more than anything, have a *reason* for it all. He did not want to believe there was no reason, no divine purpose, for his father having to live a life of suffering and then die so prematurely.

It was a bitter pill to swallow.

The funeral was in September, not long into the start of the school year. For the first time in his academic life, Nikola had begun to falter. It was completely understandable and even with his usually high level of performance diminished, he maintained an integrity that many others could only aspire to. I marvelled at my friend and his ability to remain stable. Had I been in that situation, I imagine I would have crumbled.

Nikola's father was buried in the Orthodox part of the cemetery, one towards the outskirts of town. Yet even there, on his tombstone, was engraved not a cross but a star. Free of any religious iconography, free of any words of spiritual sentimentality. This is what he would have wanted, Nikola's mother claimed. She, herself, was a religious woman, but I could see the devastation on her face that no God could bring her comfort during this time, no matter how present He was in her life.

It was a small and modest ceremony, but still a beautiful celebration of a man's life. Nikola had even summoned the strength to say a few words about his father, commending him on his strength, his artistry and his persistence throughout the years to remain committed to all that he loved most.

I could not help but cry and felt like a fool for doing so, for even Nikola managed to hold back his tears and his mother looked as if she had exhausted all of hers. I was glad to see my father stand next to Nikola's mother and squeeze her hand, not leaving her side. I was also happy to see all the family who had made it. Cousins, aunts and uncles were there, many of whom had come from neighbouring towns or cities. When I saw Nikola's uncle standing there like a statue of stone, overlooking his brother's grave, I felt a whole new lump swell up in my throat.

It was a sweet autumn day and the warmth carried on into the evening; it felt so fitting for the departure of such a loving man. The gentleness of the weather helped ease our twisted emotions, and I could see Nikola lose some of the rigidity that had overtaken his body in recent days. The symbolic act of laying a loved one to rest and saying those final goodbyes appeared to have an impact on all of us, and it became easier to start talking once more. We reminisced with Nikola and smiled at each fond memory. Soft laughter could be heard at times and slowly people began to look back fondly on a man, on an artist, and enjoy the simple pleasure of another's company.

In the months that followed the death of Nikola's father, I was so strongly relieved to see his family of two making some positive gains. Nikola had managed to organise an exhibition of his late father's work, which had immediately gained more interest, however morbidly, after the death of the locally celebrated artist. Nikola and his mother saw some profits from these sales, which helped to at least pay off the costs of the funeral. Nikola's mother took on more work after no longer having to care for her ill partner. She earned herself a promotion and her and Nikola were soon to move into a proper apartment, just for the two of them.

'Finally, God is rewarding us for all our suffering,' Nikola's mother exclaimed. I suppose that was one way to look at it. Though, it didn't answer the question of why they had to suffer in the first place.

Whether it was due to her recent test of faith or for some other unknown reason, Nikola's mother had strengthened her ties to God. In fact, she was on a first-name basis with the Creator and often felt as though He was personally assisting her through all of life's obstacles.

Nikola was not pleased by this.

'It's an insult to my father,' he said. 'He was a Godless man and he happened to die an early death. Then you have my mother, the believer, who accounts all her successes to the work of God and to her devotion to Christianity. So, are the Godless being punished?'

'Of course not,' I said in return. 'If that were the case, most of Yugoslavia would be dead.'

'You're right, it's illogical to think that way,' said Nikola. 'But I get angry at my mother when she considers all good things to be an act of God, but the death of my father—of her *husband*—was either the work of the Devil, or God working in mysterious ways. There's nothing mysterious about it. If God is responsible for killing my dad, then he's just a huge jerk.'

I laughed at this and tried to imagine how Nikola's mother would respond to such an allegation. She would probably have an answer: 'It's all part of God's plan'.

I completely understood why this infuriated Nikola. He was like me; he hated the thought of not being the master of his own destiny. What was the point of any of us, if life was nothing but some sort of game that had been fixed long ago by a single player? It seemed to me that if that were the case, then every individual on Earth would be void of all responsibility. It would not matter what we did.

These philosophical discussions only further confused Nikola and me, especially as our lives appeared absent of any objective adults capable of thinking critically and enlightening us. He had a mother with a new zest for God, whereas I had parents sworn to socialism. Whatever remnants of religion persisted in my family were so trivial they had simply lost all meaning.

But I was seeking some sort of explanation for things—for our lives and our society and what it was all for. And I didn't want the answer to come from others' interpretations of God or from Marxism.

Ana and Marko were not much help in these discussions. They were both of Catholic background, yet the general religious or spiritual knowledge of both of them combined was equivalent to that of the Pope's knowledge of quantum physics; they knew *of* it, but simply saw no purpose for it in their lives and therefore gave it no more serious thought.

Marko's parents were Catholic in their mindset and in practice, but even they did not kid themselves into thinking that their son cared for anything remotely related to churches and the Virgin Mary. Ana's parents were simply Catholic by default, as that was their background, yet I doubt either of them even knew where the nearest Catholic church was.

Marko surprised me at times with his ability to contemplate matters of life and existence. These moments were exceptionally rare, but they did occur. After the funeral of Nikola's father, I did not expect Marko to think or behave any differently, but he had somewhat changed his approach to things. He had become slightly less afraid of holding back emotions and less concerned with drawing attention to himself. I was even more amazed when Nikola admitted to me that Marko had helped him get through the experience with their shared discussions. Marko had empathy, despite what others thought. When he saw Nikola lose his father, it affected Marko. Perhaps it struck him so profoundly because Marko himself had never been close with his own father, and therefore he always had that sense of loss there, however small.

After so many years together, we now found ourselves encountering things that made us question our lives and turn to one another for support. Nikola was forced to mature considerably and quickly, and I sometimes forgot we were the same age. Marko never failed to remind us of our youth and to counter the seriousness that would sometimes consume us. Ana, too, kept me focused on the here and now and on everyone else in our lives.

Winter settled in without the usual morose feelings, because in the second month of the year the whole nation was tuned into the Winter Olympics in Sarajevo. I was so glad for this telecast, not just for the excitement it brought about, but for the distraction it provided for Nikola. He, like the rest of us, could find no excuse to dwell in the miserable conditions of the cold. Our eyes and ears were tuned in to the television at any given time, following the various events, tracking the glory and the failures of the athletes.

My favourite part was watching the torch relay. I loved to see the ecstatic faces of the crowds in all of the different cities of Yugoslavia. The opening ceremony was even better. We had all gathered at my place to watch it, and Marko broke down in fits of laughter when the Olympic flag was mistakenly raised upside down.

'That's so typical of us,' Marko said smiling, as a fresh wave of patriotism washed over his face.

Although we had already returned to school from our winter break, Nikola, Ana, Marko and I would often find ourselves rushing straight back to one of our homes and tuning into the events. And although the northern Europeans were still dominating in the winter sports, we yelled and cheered with pride at every little achievement made by our own country men and women. The greatest moment of joy came when Yugoslavia won its first and only medal, a silver one, earned by Jure Franko in the giant slalom.

Marko and I were home alone with Alisa as we watched this event take place, and we could even hear the neighbours cheering in the apartment next door to us. We spent the next hour or so discussing the highlights of the giant slalom until my parents came home, and then we regaled them with a detailed recount.

Marko came over once again to view the closing ceremony with me, and we feasted on the cakes Mama had made, with our eyes glued to the television screen. Alisa was not even six years old yet but had already developed a habit of wanting to do everything she saw, and by the end of the Winter Olympics she had set her sights on everything from skiing to sledding. I tried to explain to her that Zadar probably wasn't the best place to take up any sort of winter sport, and that she may have to settle for swimming or water polo, like just about every other kid in the city.

'Mara, don't crush her dreams already!' Marko said to me with false indignation. I scowled at him in return.

'Hey, why don't we go ice-skating while we still can?' Marko suggested.

Alisa perked up at the sound of this and I couldn't make up an excuse fast enough. I was a bit over-protective of my sister and was fearful she might hurt herself. Then, I remembered my ice-skating boots, the beautiful fur-lined ones my father had bought me years ago. Alisa would be just old enough to wear them now.

'In fact,' Marko said, 'we're going right now!' He picked up Alisa, who squealed with joy, and ran off to fetch her jacket. I sighed and went along with it. It was evening by this point, but Marko saw this as no obstacle. We made it to the ice rink set up in town and Marko convinced the operator to let us have a quick skate.

Alisa was in a wonderland. Marko took her hand in his and skated as fast as he could, while I sat there still trying to put my skates on (silently freaking out).

My sister had no fear. She picked up ice skating in the same way little kids pick up everything—with no concept of pain or failure to hinder her. Marko wasn't soft on her, either. When she did fall, he picked her back up and encouraged her to go even faster the next time.

The three of us skated until we worked up a sweat and Alisa began to cough, at which point I had to put a stop to it. Mama would kill me if Alisa came home sick after a night racing around in the cold. I don't remember the last time I'd received a wooden spoon to the butt, but I feared I was not too old to still receive such a punishment.

It took some time to calm Alisa, who was still on an adrenalin rush. We made our way home and Marko carried Alisa for the last few minutes, after her legs had finally caught on to the exhaustion her body was feeling.

We parted ways in the courtyard, and I carried Alisa back towards our apartment. I looked over at Marko who was gently strolling back home, slowly and in no rush. I wondered whether he really felt like going home at all.

Chapter 9

'If I have to watch *Indiana Jones and the Temple of Doom* one more time, I swear, I will gouge my own eyes out,' I said to Nikola as we walked out of the cinema for what I sincerely hoped was the last time that summer. I was looking forward to returning to school just so I could avoid the cinema. I actually *felt* the need to learn something.

'Tell me about it,' Nikola sighed. Nikola was an avid film watcher, but even he recognised when something was overkill. However, Marko's obsession with wanting to be Harrison Ford, alongside Ana's obsession with wanting to marry Harrison Ford, meant Nikola and I didn't get much of a say when it came to which films to watch. The one time I did manage to convince the others to go and watch *Firestarter*, Ana came out of the cinema seething at the 'waste of cinematic time'. I was too freaked out though, as the little fire-starting girl was around the same age as Alisa, and I was already making mental notes to monitor my little sister's moods more closely.

'It's decided, I'm becoming an archaeologist,' Marko declared when he and Ana finally caught up to Nikola and me. Nikola just glanced at me sideways and attempted to cover up his smirk. I did not even bother explaining to Marko what the real work of archaeologists might look like, as I could see he was revelling in his fantasy.

'And I'm going to travel to India!' Ana announced. At this point, Nikola's face turned from amusement into confusion.

'What part of watching a man get his heart ripped out from his chest in some bizarre ritual ceremony makes you want to go to India?' he said.

'Not to mention how incredibly untrue that whole scenario is,' I added. 'I don't think any culture would glorify—'

'Will you two just stop! You just don't understand,' Ana said with a swish of her ponytail, instantly dismissing our rebuttals. I decided to give up on her, too. Ana went back to talking to Marko, the only person sharing her enthusiasm.

'You know, it could've been worse,' Nikola said to me quietly. 'They could have discovered *Conan the Destroyer* instead, and we would've had to watch *that* film a thousand times. Can you even imagine?' I erupted into laughter and gave my friend a pat on the back.

The best part about the four of us back then, was that there was always at least one other person who got you. I never felt misunderstood, and I was never alone. That's probably why, despite my complaints, I was willing to watch the same adventure film countless times over. That's what friends are for. And anyway, I knew within a matter of months, the next new obsession would come along (it did—*The Terminator*, and we had to watch Schwarzenegger after all) and our imaginations would set us free once again.

Being in middle school, it was like standing on the precipice of independence and responsibility but not yet needing to jump. It was all action films and rock'n'roll music, jetty diving and street soccer. It was laughter in the classroom, only to be rudely interrupted by schoolwork. It was growth spurts over the holidays, experimental hairstyles and regrettable fashion choices. Yet we grew alongside each other and as individuals, like one of the many vines found along our coastline, forever overlapping and intertwining, but always connected at the roots.

A bowl of *Smoki* lay strewn across the floor. All traces of the earlier day's chocolate supply were gone, otherwise melted onto the aluminium wrapping. Two empty bottles of lemonade and a half-full carton of apricot juice haphazardly littered the small space between the sofa and the television set, perilously close to becoming the catalyst for a spectacular fall.

But Marko's feet miraculously seemed to avoid all the junk surrounding him. His upper half was even more animated in an aggressive display of swinging arms and jerking torso; if he wasn't being so vocal, it would have appeared as though he were a most talented actor of the silent film genre. Alas, his mouth seemed to be doing the most work of all: releasing every possible expletive and groan, all in the direction of the television set.

I could not blame him—I was feeling it too, although I had found a way of containing my emotions. I knew right then that half of Zadar was taking part in the mentally draining and physically exhausting activity that was watching a basketball championship. Zadar had made it to the 1986 finals and were facing off Cibona. The torture had been further prolonged by the match going into second overtime. Nikola was silently mesmerised by the television set and had managed to chew off all ten of his fingernails. If he kept going at this rate, he was going to hit bone.

Tata kept walking in and out of the living room, partly due to his inability to handle such a high-stress situation, and partly due to his intolerance of Marko's commentary. Even Mama was on the edge of her seat, quite literally, sitting by the kitchen table and not daring to look at the television screen.

What happened then and there was unforgettable. In the last moments of the match, one point down, Zadar managed to hit a shot and score two points. It finished 111 to 110. I did not even have time to register my excitement before Marko let out a shout equivalent to that of an ancient war cry, and finally, *inevitably*, put his right foot onto one of the empty bottles. Resembling a real-time slow-motion movie, he came crashing down onto his back. The rest of us were too busy celebrating to help him up, and chose instead to pile on top of him, a mess of bodies and cheering and laughing and tears.

That evening, the town was predictably full of basketball fans who refused to cease their celebrations. The team colours could be seen on every sidewalk and street, hanging out of the windows of homes and businesses. I allowed myself to relax and to celebrate alongside my townspeople, for I knew that over the coming two months I would be deeply engrossed in my schooling. But right then, I could experience the ecstasy of victory and a reawakened sense of pride towards my hometown.

It was Aleksandar who threw the after-party, as was the custom. His house was the nicest and his parents the most accommodating. By the time word got around about Aleksandar's party, it was already late, but people were still in high spirits as they turned up. Marko and I arrived with a fresh supply of drinks, having already consumed a few beers beforehand. This was a new venture for us, so it didn't take much for the drinks to have an effect.

Surprisingly enough, it was Nikola who was the most celebratory of all. He was a huge basketball fan at heart, so he was probably the happiest out of all of us.

Ana arrived not long after, with a few other girls from school. I was amazed to see that even she was wearing the basketball jersey of Zadar. Ana, who had no understanding of competitive sport, looked like a dedicated fan who turned up to matches with a painted face and an insatiable thirst for victory. Then I remembered she also harboured a massive crush for Petar Popović, Zadar's star shooter and game-winner. Her love for him was cemented after tonight.

Dalmatian music was blaring from the stereo, with everyone singing in uncharacteristic harmony for a bunch of over-tired and over-stimulated youths. This went on long enough for most of us to forget what we were even celebrating. Then, it had to end when Aleksandar's father came downstairs and begged us to stop.

'Some of us still have jobs to wake up to, you know!' he exclaimed in a tired but understanding tone. 'Now, if you have no safe way of getting home, just sleep here. And please ... don't tell your parents about this.'

We all agreed that Aleksandar had the best father ever, then proceeded to find the closest soft surface to crash down on.

I woke up quite early, it seemed, to the sound of Aleksandar's father reversing the car out of the driveway. What an injustice, I thought. My head was throbbing, but it was bearable enough. I felt like I could drink five litres of water in one go.

I looked beside me to see Marko's feet almost poking into my face. We'd fallen asleep on the couch, his head on one side and mine on the other. He was lying there so peacefully that I had to stare closely to make sure he was still breathing. He was still fully dressed, and as I studied the Levis jeans he wore, I found myself thinking how I didn't know anyone else who looked quite so good in a pair of jeans (apart from Bruce Springsteen). As quickly as I had thought it, I attempted to banish it from my mind. It must had been the influence of alcohol that allowed my thoughts to wander into such foolish territory.

I waited for Marko to wake up, and when he did, we walked home together, letting the fresh air sober us up.

Apart from that night's regrettable venture into alcohol consumption, I had made a conscious effort to prioritise my studies over all else. And when that final paper was written and the last school day was over, immense relief engulfed me.

Fortunately for me, the results had been positive. I had done better than I thought and had been accepted into the *gimnazija* high school I wanted, the same one as Ana and Nikola.

But of course, there was a downside. Marko had, unsurprisingly, failed to get into the *gimnazija*. He had not wanted to even attempt it at all but was forced into applying by his parents. He got into the trade school for machinery instead, which was known for being the lowest on the scale of prestige. Marko himself was not fazed by this, especially as he knew that this was at least something he could succeed in. But the shame of having to deal with his parents' disappointment certainly did not help his mood.

I assured my friend that it did not matter; he was doing what made him happy and he would probably have a far better time at school than the rest of us would, seeing as we'd be pushed to the limits in terms of our study loads. Most importantly, we wouldn't let this interfere with our continuing friendship.

'Yeah, I guess you're right,' Marko admitted. 'It will all work out. I just have to give my parents a few months to accept that their son is no genius.'

He cast his eyes downwards and I couldn't be sure of what his expression was. 'Sometimes, I just wish I was smart,' he said. 'My life would be so much easier if I was smart.'

I didn't know how to respond to this. Marko wasn't academically gifted, but he possessed another kind of intelligence. I had a feeling that he just wasn't interested in the sorts of things that were taught at school, and that if he really wanted to, he could excel. But Marko needed to really love something to be good at it.

'Let's go out,' I said, knowing this was the best proposition I could make. I could see any shred of self-doubt that previously enveloped him disappear at the idea. It was summertime after all— our favourite time of year.

Marko was in the mood for something shallow. We bypassed our usual café of choice and went instead for the *kafana* in town that played the kind of folk music that one could only listen to whilst drunk on *rakija*. It was a little secret of ours. No one else knew of Marko's and my hidden shame. It did not occur often, but every once in a while, we felt susceptible to the likes of old Balkan songs that sang of lost loves and passionate nights in the *kafana*. We never had a problem getting into these shady spots (no one seemed fazed by the sight of young teenagers in this particular bar), but usually had a problem getting out. Marko would either not want to leave or would be forced to leave due to some foolish behaviour.

It was a cool and breezy evening, but the air inside the *kafana* was stuffy and suffocating. Smoke had consumed the entire space so that it appeared as though a thick blanket of fog had floated indoors. Marko went straight to the bar, just in time for his favourite singer to come on, Dzej Ramadanovski. If Nikola were here, he would be doubting our friendship, if not disowning us entirely. But tonight, it did not matter. It was just Marko and me, and the plum brandy was in abundance. I managed to try only a little bit of it before choosing to be responsible and turning instead to drinking lemonade. But Marko was no stranger to alcohol, and therefore helped himself to multiple servings. I found myself thinking about how easily swayed I was by Marko. It probably wasn't good for me, but I loved every moment of it.

We were into the second half of the eighties when my years as a high school student were just taking off. It was a time of new wave music, of punk and rock; of a country possibly opening up a little more to the rest of the world. But I still had my summers in the *selo*. That would never change.

My feet had developed padding on their soles that only ever appeared after much time was spent navigating one's way through rocks and stones and pebbles of all shapes and sizes. With every placement of my foot I held my breath, thanking the soft, rounded pebbles which provided relief, then cursing the ones that speared into me like little knives. It had only taken a few days at the *selo* for my mind to switch on and remember to signal to my legs and feet, *yes, I know this environment*. Now I was like Tarzan at home in his jungle.

That summer's ritual involved waking up each day to the scorching heat (and not out of free will but from the inability to handle the stagnant air any longer) and to make the journey to Nikola's place. I would have a quick breakfast of fruit and yogurt—it was too hot for anything dry or solid—and slip into my canvas shoes and walk out the door.

I knew each trail; every hilltop's curve; every house and who lived there. I knew where I was based on my view of the sea below; I knew which season we were in based on the kind of wind that was blowing.

I wished for a breeze, but there was no wind at this time of day, in the middle of summer. Nikola wasn't exactly close by; we were in a village, but the rockiness of Velebit made for an unforgivable landscape at times. It did wonders for one's leg muscles—perhaps that's why I had inherited such strong legs myself? Was it some sort of genetic predisposition that had evolved after so many generations had traipsed through these mountains and this coastline?

I plundered on, contemplating about my legs and desiring something more *feminine*, whilst little beads of sweat began to develop on my forehead. My skin had turned a golden brown, my hairs tinged to a white-blonde colour, and the hair on my head a considerable two or three shades lighter. I appeared to be blending into the surface of the earth as the sun wielded its power over this part of the planet.

I made it to Nikola's house, relieved that he was right by the water. That was where I found him, too, sitting on the shoreline and digging into a watermelon.

'Perfect timing,' I said and took a seat next to him. He handed me a large slice of watermelon, nice and cold, straight out of the fridge.

'I swear, it's as though I just hold a piece of food up in the air and you seem to appear out of nowhere, every time,' he said. I laughed and gave him a punch in the arm.

'Marko's not here so you're playing the smart arse?' I said. He gave me a sideways look of mock offense and turned back to his watermelon.

We sat together in the morning sun and devoured half a watermelon together. This was also part of the summer ritual. I thought to myself about how many more watermelons Nikola had stored in his house and where they all came from. I chuckled out loud at the thought of rooms and rooms full of watermelons, forgetting I wasn't alone. Nikola just looked at me and shook his head; he looked too hot to be bothered about me losing my senses.

The radio was turned on inside and Nikola's mother appeared in the doorway.

'Are you staying for lunch, Mara?' she called out.

'That's the only reason she's here!' Nikola replied, before I had a chance to get a word in. I didn't bother arguing. I just looked at his mother, put my hands up and shrugged, as though to say, *he's absolutely right.*

I won't say no to a seafood barbecue.

Nikola's mother began preparing the fish that Nikola had caught the previous day.

'I'm sorry, but could it be any fresher? This won't do for me.' I joked with Nikola. He grabbed the barbecue tongs and tried to pinch my arm, but I jumped out of his way.

'So, seeing as you're so full of energy, would you mind going inside and grabbing us something to drink?'

'Sure thing,' I said.

I brought a drink out for Nikola and helped myself to some of the sour cherry juice as well. Eventually, Nikola's family started turning up; his uncle came around, and then his cousins, and eventually I was bringing out enough drinks for a football team.

Nikola's family probably made up half the population of the *selo*. I only really had my great uncle left, and when I thought about it, it was only my sister and I who remained to carry on the family name.

I had asked my father once, 'Tata, how come Uncle Dmitar never had kids? He could have given you some cousins.'

Tata looked at me as though he was studying me, trying to calculate my thoughts. He must have concluded they were innocent enough, for he chose to answer me.

'Mara, Uncle Dmitar *did* have a child. He had a son who was a few years older than me. I do not remember him though.'

I looked at Tata curiously, waiting for him to carry on. When he didn't, I had to ask the obvious question. 'Well? What happened to him?'

Tata gave me that look again, contemplating how to answer my question, or whether it was worth an answer at all.

'He died, Mara,' my father finally revealed. 'When he was only a small child.'

Again, I had to prompt him, although I was growing cautious now. 'How?' I asked.

'Uncle Dmitar used to live in the city with his wife and child,' my father said. This caught me by surprise, as I had not even given thought to a possible wife. It made sense though.

'Anyway,' Tata continued. 'They lived in an apartment block of only a few storeys, with very little room. Dmitar's wife worked most of the time, but Dmitar had a hard time finding jobs. He was not in a good place, so he drank a lot. Too much. One day, he was meant to be taking care of his boy while his wife was at work. She had told him to mind the pot of boiling water on the stove, which she was using to wash the bed sheets. But I guess Dmitar was in no state to be mindful. The little boy was left unattended as he reached for the pot and pulled it over the top of himself. Dmitar only realised something was wrong when he heard the screaming coming from the kitchen. He managed to rush the boy to hospital, but it was too late. His son died from the burns.'

My father looked at me carefully, as though afraid he had traumatised me with this story.

'What was his name?' I asked.

'The boy? His name was Ivan.'

'What happened after that?'

'As you can probably imagine, Dmitar's wife never forgave him. Dmitar never forgave himself either, and after separating from his wife he returned to the *selo* and began living the life of solitude which he still leads to this day. At least his excessive drinking stopped.'

I appreciated my father's honesty that day. It is something I could always count on. He didn't like to hide things from me; he always gave me a straight answer to serious questions. I think I knew from an early age how lucky I was, so I always treated the knowledge he imparted to me as a valuable gift.

Tata was good to his uncle. He spent many of his summers at the *selo* as well, where he helped Dmitar maintain the property. They would prepare lunch together during the day and play cards in the evenings. Dmitar loved it most when Mama would come with Alisa. This was when Dmitar would pick up my sister, give her a big hug, and somehow have the nerve and patience to put up with the constant demands of a child all day. Alisa had that effect on people—the cute little one, still a novelty. Or maybe Dmitar still had a lot of love to give.

Chapter 10

Algebra. Latin. Geometry. Ancient history. Biology. Just listing all the subjects I had to study for required a large amount of effort. Literature. Chemistry. Philosophy. I was still not sure of what I wanted to focus on, let alone 'what I wanted to be when I grew up'. The natural world seemed to make the most sense to me, and there was something I found incredibly appealing about the possibility of discovery. Latin, however, left me feeling as dead as the language itself.

'Sweet Jesus,' Marko said to me when he laid his eyes upon the textbooks I had bought for the upcoming school year. He had invited himself over on the pretence of helping me prepare my materials for high school, but we both knew that was a lie.

'Thank you for reaffirming my decision *not* to go to your school,' he said. I was about to say to him that it wasn't his decision, seeing as he didn't actually get into my school, but I held back. Marko didn't need me to remind him of that.

'It's not so bad,' I said to him. 'As long as I get good teachers this year. You remember last year when we got stuck with Professor Stefanovski for history? As though the subject's not dry enough as it is. At least he wasn't frightening, though. That maths teacher who came and took over the class was a *witch*. Ana trembled every time she got called up to do an equation on the board.'

'She didn't scare me. I was definitely her favourite,' Marko said.
'Oh yeah, how do you know?'

'Look at my gorgeous face! No woman alive could resist it,' he replied. I grabbed the closest textbook and hit him across the head with *Biology, 3rd edition*. He laughed it off, feeling quite proud of himself.

I sighed and asked if he wanted a coffee.

'Sure, I'll have one. Just skip the sugar thanks. I don't want any breakouts on my skin. My beauty is my livelihood.' He laughed at his own joke once more and I went into the kitchen to brew us some Turkish coffee, which I intended to make with a decent amount of sugar in it, of course.

Yet again, I found my priorities taking a back seat as Marko grabbed at my attention. I'd always been too readily accepting of Marko infiltrating all my plans and good intentions.

I finished making the coffee and brought it into the living room. Marko sat up from his seat where he had been flicking through last week's newspaper, a copy of *Weekly Dalmatia*. My father and I had taken to reading the paper recently, if only for the political satire supplement that came with it every week. Marko always teased me for having an interest in such 'boring' literature, but I countered that only ever reading the TV guide was pretty low-level, even for him.

'Marko, I didn't know you could read,' I said as he put the paper down. He grabbed it again and rolled it up, motioning to hit me across the head with it.

'Don't be silly, you know I was only looking at the pictures,' he replied.

We both took a sip of our coffee and relaxed for a moment, enjoying the silence. Then a loud knocking on the door made us both jump, and I spilled a bit of the hot coffee onto my hand, swearing out loud.

'Marko!' his father's voice boomed through the wooden door. 'If you think I'm finished with you, think again!' Marko had gone pale, but he got up immediately.

'I'm coming!' he yelled back through the door. Marko gave me a sheepish look and muttered an apology. His ears were burning red.

'Hey, it's ok,' I attempted to say coolly. 'You better go, we'll talk soon.'

Marko opened the door and slid out without giving me a chance to see anything. I heard his and his father's footsteps dissipate, only to be interrupted by some more of his father's shouting. I hoped everything was ok.

I walked back into my silent living room. Not sure of what to do, I took the coffee back into the kitchen and poured it down the drain. I guess I had no excuse now not to study. But I'd lost all motivation the moment the front door closed behind Marko.

Gimnazija Jurja Barakovića was located on the half-island, *Poluotok*. It wasn't really a longer walk than it had been to my primary school, but it was certainly lonelier. For the first time, Marko and I would not be going to the same school.

'You've still got me!' Alisa shouted with far more enthusiasm than I was feeling. It was true though. I still had to walk with her to the primary school and drop her off, then go down the road to my high school. She used to just tag along behind Marko and me, but now I could tell she was excited to have my full attention.

I reminded myself that as strange as it felt for me, Marko must have felt even worse. He would know hardly anyone at his new school. When I expressed my worries for Marko to Ana, she seemed surprised.

'Marko could make friends with a fire hydrant, Mara! Why are you worried for him? If anything, you should be worried that he'll forget all about us!' I hated how she knew my fears better than I did. But Ana was only half-right in her assertion. Marko did indeed go on to make friends easily at his new school, but he most definitely did not forget about us.

He was standing in front of *Gimnazija Jurja Barakovića* one day after school had finished. I saw Marko talking and laughing with Nikola before Nikola left to go home. I said bye to Ana, who was going straight to her piano lesson, and I headed towards Marko. 'And, what brings you here on this fine day?' I asked.

Marko flashed me his signature smirk, indicating that he had surely done something not entirely innocent. 'I skipped my last lesson to come and meet you, so we could walk home together. We've been in high school for long enough already and I figured I got the hang of things by now,' he exclaimed.

'Is that so?' I said. 'So, you're pretty much ready to graduate?'

'Pretty much. I reckon life's not that hard to figure out.'

'You'll have to teach me everything you know.' I did my most sarcastic voice.

'There's not enough time in the world for that,' he retorted. 'Geniuses are born, not made,' he said as he lost his footing and tripped over a tree root. We both laughed and I zipped my jacket up a bit higher, braving the cold as we went on our way.

I knew Marko couldn't afford to miss any lessons. Someone like Nikola certainly could (not that he *ever* would), but Marko was used to making his own rules. I didn't lecture him about it though. How could I, when I was happy to have his company?

'We have to go get Alisa first,' I said to Marko. 'She's probably already waiting for me.' We sped up into a brisk walk as the cool wind blowing from across the sea whipped around our heads.

I shot a glance at Marko as we walked, and I noticed bruises on his neck. I wasn't sure if he knew I was looking, but he quickly zipped his jacket up higher and buried his face downwards against the wind. Even if I had asked him about the bruises, I knew he would have made up some excuse. But I never asked. Looking back, I wondered whether things would have been different if I had at least tried talking to him about those uncomfortable truths. But those sorts of things just weren't discussed. And anyway, I knew it was better to be polite than honest.

"Marko!" Alisa cried as we approached her school. Marko pulled her in for a one-armed hug and we set off, all three of us, back towards our apartment blocks. Alisa wasn't usually very chatty whenever I came to pick her up, but with Marko here, she couldn't stop reciting her day's events. I felt like even though Marko had wanted to walk home with me, he was entertaining Alisa's stories with more enthusiasm than usual, as though he welcomed the distraction. Perhaps he was as scared as I was about facing the question that neither of us wanted to hear the answer to.

After that day, Marko skipped classes less and less. Maybe he wanted to avoid the possibility of me questioning him, or perhaps he just realised he had to focus on school and stop getting into trouble. But by the end of our first year of high school, I couldn't see any more bruises on his neck. Or maybe they were just hidden away on some other part of his body.

The Maraska factory, our pride and joy, was nothing but noticeable on the shoreline of Zadar—a major source of income for our city and also the source of our beverages, non-alcoholic and alcoholic alike. *Maraschino*—which we always had at the ready in our kitchen cabinet—and sour cherry syrup—my personal favourite, which refreshed like nothing else could during the summertime. Maraska made a variety of juices and were famous for their Dalmatian spirits. But somehow, spending my summer in the factory felt a lot less enjoyable than consuming their products.

Ana and I had carefully deliberated and finally decided that a summer job was a good idea. We had survived our first year of high school and were ready for the next great venture. We would earn a solid amount of cash, which we would then waste on materialistic items. It sounded like a great plan. Ana said she was planning to go to Italy before school started again to get herself a pair of new Levis 501s. I wasn't so sure what I had planned, but I wanted money. So, she and I got some work at Maraska, where her father worked in accounting.

It was physical and monotonous work, but more painful was having to watch all our friends relish their freedom, spending their days lying in the sun or swimming in the sea. I myself felt as though I was slowly being put off my favourite sour cherry drink, for the smell of it had permanently settled in my nostrils. But I kept reminding myself of the money, and as the weeks went by, I allowed myself to slack off a little bit. Ana was under more pressure though, as she had to make sure nothing negative was mentioned to her father. She took her job seriously, filling up bottles and crates, doing the most she could. I admired her work ethic, but not enough to adopt it.

We had accumulated a decent amount of money over the course of our days and nights slaving away at the factory. I put my money aside and intended to spend it on some sort of trip somewhere. Ana did just as she said she would and invested in her beloved Levis, as well as half of the fashion on offer in Trieste, where she spent the final week of her school break. All of those earnings gone so quickly, and Ana couldn't have been happier. I, being the best friend, promised that I'd be borrowing all her new clothes at any given point in time. That's what friends are for, after all.

Marko had also made himself useful, to an extent, and had developed some solid earnings over the summer. Yet, he had done so not through hard work, but through competing. Marko had spent much of the summer visiting the prime tourist destinations of our town and beyond, going as far north as Pula at one stage, and challenging any willing tourist to a match of tennis. The unsuspecting foreigner would often agree, and the bets would be placed. Marko was a natural sportsman and always won, therefore it didn't take long for him to accumulate a small fortune.

'But what happens if you lose?' I had asked him. 'You don't actually have any of your own money, so how would you pay for the bet?'

'Simple,' Marko replied. 'I just make sure not to lose.'

And it really was that simple for him. If he was up for more of a challenge, he sometimes played one-on-one basketball with the tourists, or raced them from one point in the sea to another. Even then, Marko never lost. He travelled quite far at times, always leaving without any money, and always returning with a profit. And as an added bonus, he was keeping incredibly fit.

Everyone had managed to do some kind of travelling, yet I still had my savings intact. But I wasn't savouring the prospect of another winter spent in my sleepy coastal town.

Apart from his visits to Belgrade, which coincided with our own, I could not recall even one occasion in which we had visited our great uncle, Miki. '*Sramota*,' my mother would say. For shame.

'Now when are you going to come and visit us up here, ej, *Dalmatinci*?' He would always invite us to visit, and naturally, we would always promise to do so. But life has its way of moving on quickly without stopping, and often years can go by without notice. It was after a call from Uncle Miki, during which he regaled me with his jokes and stories, that I decided to become a little more active in fulfilling, so far, empty promises. I felt ashamed that I was so distant from so much of my family when nothing but a few rivers and mountains separated us.

I took the money saved from my summer earnings at the Maraska factory and used it to purchase a bus ticket to Osijek, from where I crossed into Serbia, to the town of Apatin. On the outskirts of the town was Uncle Miki's farm, which I suspected would be covered in a fine layer of snow by this point.

A smoked pig on a spit greeted me upon arrival, ready to be shaved into strips of prosciutto. I was worried at first that I had underestimated the cold, but the food that Miki and his family provided me with was enough to warm up Antarctica. Miki had an old Renault in which the heating did not work, meaning the car ride from the bus station to his farm was a test of survival. But whatever he may have lacked in technology and material goods, Miki made up for in good food and drinks.

Miki's son, Tomo, greeted me with a huge smile on his face. Tomo was excited, since he didn't receive very many visitors in Apatin. Uncle Branislav had made the journey up north and Aunt Dragana had visited more often since she moved to Belgrade, but my own mother had hardly ever come so far to see her uncle and cousin.

'I can't blame you city folk. I know how busy your lives get,' Miki said to me. 'Just remind yourself every now and then that life is passing by without you even taking notice.'

Miki was the philosopher who had advice for everything and everyone, without so much as having left his town. I had to admit though, he was quite worldly for someone so connected to his roots.

Miki and Tomo had a lot of neighbours, who came and went as they pleased without any announcement. It was good to see, as it ensured they still maintained contact with other people. Their home was always tidy and warm. Apart from the lingering smell of smoked meat and goat cheese, it was very comfortable.

My ignorant self quickly came to learn just how busy farm life really was. The farmers were in constant negotiation with each other, so the image I had conjured of an isolated hermitical existence completely evaporated from my mind. Miki and Tomo appeared to be more popular than I was, and I came to love the action that was always taking place around the property.

On the one day when no one had actually come to visit us, I worried that something had happened. 'Everyone needs their rest, even us workers of the land,' Miki rationalised. The following day, the guests arrived once more. One needed help with a stubborn goat, the other had a cow that he suspected was falling ill and was seeking advice for, and one visitor from the house in the next paddock had come by with a crate load of smoked sausages. Miki accepted them with gratitude, despite already having an attic full of his own smoked sausages. Apparently, there could never be enough of them.

I helped out where and when I could, but essentially, I was useless when it came to farm chores. Instead, I waited for the snow to pile up and then shovelled it, and when there was enough I would make a few snowmen. I employed the assistance of Tomo after a particularly snowy day, and we managed to make a two-metre-tall snowman. We gave him a hat and a smoked sausage for a nose.

Great Uncle Miki would honour us with several renditions of Partizan war songs most nights. Tomo would sometimes join in. I would sit back and smile politely after the eighth time of hearing 'Bella Ciao' sung in Miki's baritone vocals. It only took a few more nights until I too had memorised each song, and then I finally felt brave enough to join them. Miki loved it.

Inevitably, each singing session was followed by a history lesson (albeit a very subjective one). Uncle Miki was a born storyteller, and it was fair to say he favoured the genre of 'war history'. Miki had an endless supply of stories from his days spent resisting fascist aggression during World War Two. He spoke of countless battles and victories on the front, several of which involved our very own late president, Marshall Tito. Uncle Miki was on first-name basis with Marshall Tito, sometimes referring to him as *Josip*, although I questioned whether Tito was ever aware of this. Naturally, I did not express my doubts to Great Uncle Miki, so as not to tarnish his memories.

'The war was where he got the nickname, *Tito*, comrade Josip,' Miki had said. 'And with that name he created a legacy!'

I wanted to ask my uncle what President Tito had been like as a man, but I feared I wouldn't get a very thorough or even-handed answer. I already knew he would have been brave, honourable and a true believer in socialism and justice. That's the version Uncle Miki would have given me. I, however, was more interested in what Tito's favourite food was, what kind of books he read, whether he made any jokes or if he had a particular smell to him. Ultimately, it wasn't important. I was satisfied with Miki's version of people and events, for in his world, there was always a clear distinction between good and bad. There were those who fought for justice, and those who perpetrated injustices, and everything else was of less importance.

After staying with Miki and Tomo for ten days, I felt as though I had put on several kilos of pure fat, and perhaps a little bit of muscle from shovelling so much snow. I figured if I was a little more hands-on, then maybe my physical work would counteract all the eating I was doing.

'You can tell you're a city kid, but there's workers' blood running through your veins. Partizan blood!' And with that comment, he gave me the old Partizan salute. I gave one in return, for by now the gesture had become almost a habit.

From Great Uncle Miki, I had a renewed supply of war stories, and from Tomo I had an extra suitcase full of preserved food. I sincerely hoped that no one on the bus ride back would need to check my luggage, for it would look as if I was planning on going into hiding from an apocalyptic war. I knew my parents would be happy though, for no one would be so foolish as to ignore the value of home-produced village food—the healthiest and the tastiest of all the foods.

Chapter II

I watched the sweat glistening from Tata's brow as he heaved the wooden ladder back into Uncle Dmitar's shed. They had finally finished the fixing, painting, weeding and pruning that that house demanded each year. Usually they would get a move on while it was still spring time, or at least early summer, but it was left too late and the scorching heat settled in earlier than usual this season. It made for difficult working conditions.

Tata returned from the shed, still sweating. He walked straight past where I was sitting on the concrete jetty and dived into the water, resurfacing many metres away from the shore. I let out a laugh, having been taken by surprise.

'Jump in, my daughter!' Tata called out. I could tell he was in the mood for mischief. I knew if I joined him, he'd tickle me or dunk me under the surface or pull some other sort of trick. No thanks.

'I'm not falling for it that easily!' I yelled out, with my feet dangling over the water's edge. Tata shrugged and dived back under the water, leaving only bubbles in his wake. Uncle Dmitar came out of the house at that moment, carrying two cold beers.

'Where's my nephew disappeared to?' he asked me. But before I could answer, Tata emerged from the water right in front of me, and I let out a tremendous scream as he grabbed me and pulled me into the sea with him.

'TATA!' I yelled once I finally came up for air. I was laughing of course, but feigning annoyance nonetheless.

'*Hajde, hajde,*' Tata said. Come on. *Toughen up.*

The water felt amazing once I recovered from the shock. I swam towards Tata to catch him but he slipped away effortlessly. He was a master swimmer. For such a giant man, he moved gracefully in the water. I swam back to the jetty and pulled myself back up, the salty water dripping down my hair and into my mouth. I took a seat next to Uncle Dmitar and poured myself a glass of mineral water.

I could see Tata some distance away, having decided to go for a proper swim. He often did laps across the shoreline, swimming past our neighbours and stopping to say hello to the locals. Uncle Dmitar appeared content. He was sipping away at his beer, satisfied with the work that was done and happy to unwind in the summer heat.

Mama and Alisa had left for Sarajevo only days before to visit Branislav and Selma, and their new baby girl, Lejla. I was supposed to go with them but I could tell that Baka Anka and Dida Ilija were desperate to go too, so I told Mama to take them with her. Four people in the Fiat was plenty, and I preferred to spend a hot summer in the *selo* anyway, rather than inland. My grandparents rarely ventured very far so they were excited for the trip. And as Branislav was their youngest and only son, welcoming *his* first child was quite a big occasion.

Which left Tata and me. We left Zadar almost immediately, and by the time we reached the *selo*, it was already full of visitors and travellers.

'Doesn't anyone work anymore?' I asked Uncle Dmitar. There appeared to be more and more people here, all of whom seemed to be taking longer holidays.

'Probably not,' said Dmitar, in all seriousness. 'Productivity has dropped right off, and indifference has taken over. If I didn't benefit from all the tourism, I'd be worried.' He said all this as though he knew something I didn't.

Eventually I spotted a dot in the water that grew larger and larger as it came closer to us, until my dad reappeared in his full form and finally got out of the sea.

'Dmitar, why didn't you join me?' Tata asked his uncle.

'Stop making fun of me. You know I could never keep up with you,' Dmitar replied as Tata chuckled. 'Besides, at my age one can't even sleep anymore without sustaining some sort of injury.' As the two men made light conversation, I crept away into the house and got changed. Of all the people in the *selo*, there was only one friend I was still waiting for. Nikola was supposed to arrive today, and I could hardly wait.

When I saw Nikola jump out of his mother's car along with Ana and Marko, I couldn't help but be reminded of those comedy skits where multiple clowns exit a ludicrously small car. I was almost holding out to see more people come out of the car, alas, it was only my three friends. Though, this was not a disappointment at all.

'Surprise!' Ana announced, throwing her arms up. I laughed and gave my friend a big hug, then did the same to Nikola and Marko. Marko gave me an extra-large pat on the back too, followed by a wink.

'I thought we could allow these two vagrants some time in our precious *selo*, what do you think, Mara?' Nikola asked.

'I suppose so, but only if they remain on their best behaviour and honour and respect our high-profile status,' I replied.

'Wow, queen of the village,' Marko said sarcastically. 'I am not worthy!'

'Oh please,' I said back to him. 'Don't pretend you're not a little show-off every time you cross over to your grandmother's island, her little golden boy.' Marko made to grab me but I jumped out of his way.

'Hey, one day that whole island will be mine, you'll see,' Marko said. He stretched out his arms and raised his face towards the sun, absorbing its delicious glow and letting the warmth settle into his skin. Ana was already unloading her bags and looking at me.

'Well? Am I going to get a chance to sunbake before the sun sets today? Let's go! I'm staying at your place, and I need to get changed!' Ana stated.

'Meet you at your place, yeah?' Nikola said to me whilst casting a pitying gaze in my direction.

'You bet. See you soon.' I picked up Ana's second bag and we began the walk back towards Uncle Dmitar's house.

'How was the drive here?' I asked her.

'Yeah fine, Nikola drives like an old woman.' Ana said, smiling at me.

'In no way whatsoever does that surprise me,' I said.

'Marko was a bit quiet though,' she added. I gave her a quizzical look and asked whether anything had happened.

'Nothing happened, but you know Marko. Sometimes he seems a bit vacant. Goes to a dark and distant place.'

'What?' I asked, genuinely confused. 'I don't think I've ever experienced that side of him. *Our* Marko?'

'Well I guess it's hard to see, especially cause he's so upbeat whenever you're around. But it's different when you're not there. Believe me. Ask Nikola.' Ana said.

As we approached Uncle Dmitar's house, the waves could be heard gently lapping at the jetty. I strained to remember a time when Marko's behaviour had worried me. I knew I had to ask Nikola about what Ana had told me. It just didn't add up.

But somehow, as we slipped into holiday mode and the summer sun shone all our worries away, I let myself give in to the lulling waters and the comfort of my friends' company. I watched Marko do backflips off the jetty while Nikola turned up the radio to '*Igra Rock'n'Roll cela Jugoslavija*', the pop-rock anthem providing the perfect backdrop to what felt like another day in paradise.

After yet another painfully slow school year, we reached the autumn of 1989 and the final academic hurdle. This year, I promised to myself, there would be no fooling around. I was going to be the perfect example of a student. One hundred percent attendance, all assignments completed on time, all test scores aced. I had spent the past year fumbling my way through, perhaps prioritising social events over study sessions, and I was worried I had set myself back.

I was mildly jealous of Ana, who, even while maintaining a social life, seemed to flawlessly move through her education with little effort. I on the other hand had the attention span of a three-year-old.

It was precisely at that moment, as I sat in the living room with the TV muted, restlessly planning my final year of high school in the afternoon heat, that I received a phone call from Marko.

'Let's go out,' he said.

'I can't,' I replied. 'I'm trying to study.'

'Study? School hasn't even started yet!'

'Yes, but I'm trying to get a head start this time, seeing as I didn't do so the last eleven years.'

'Do I have the wrong number? Hello? Mara?'

I mustered a laugh despite having minimal energy.

'No, it is I. Mara Marinković, the girl who has the unfortunate pleasure of being your friend,' I answered.

'Har-har-har. Very funny. I'm coming over, you better have ice-cream in the freezer. It is hot as hell today.' And with that, he hung up the phone.

With feigned annoyance, I closed my diary and notebooks. Naturally, I was relieved to have an excuse to stop studying, but I couldn't let that show, not even to myself. After all, as of now I was an exemplary student.

I went to the kitchen and opened the freezer, checking to make sure that our ice-cream supply would be enough to sustain Marko for the afternoon. With only half a tub of chocolate and vanilla swirl left in the freezer, I worried that my friend, with an insatiable desire for frozen dairy products, would be left unsatisfied. I grabbed two glasses from the cupboard and filled them with cold, refreshing *Cockta—the Drink of Our Youth*—from the fridge. The delicious dark liquid fizzed pleasantly as I dropped a couple of ice cubes into each glass. I heard the doorbell ring downstairs and went to push the button on the receiver, letting Marko in.

'Gimme, gimme, gimme,' he said, gesturing towards the cold drink in my hand. I gave him a glass and he guzzled half of it down, letting out a charming belch at the end of it.

'So where do you suggest we go, oh wise one, in this scorching heat?' I asked him.

'Antarctica. Or perhaps even the moon.'

'Excellent choice.'

We sat on the sofa, drinking our *Cockta* and saying nothing, content with the flickering images on the muted TV. This is what I liked most about being with Marko; not having to say anything. He was my go-to friend for everything, including doing nothing. I watched him from the corner of my eye, his mouth hanging open ungraciously, taking deep, slow breaths to combat the warmth. He had become more tolerable as he had grown older. He was still far from mature, but he had made progress in bounds and leaps, that was for sure.

'What century are you living in? Do you even own an air conditioner?' he said. I rolled my eyes, any warm feelings towards him subsiding.

'No, we usually get the slaves to fan us, but they're down in the slaves' quarters right now, next to the harem.'

'Well they should be working. Maybe you're not whipping them hard enough.'

'Point taken. Thanks for the tip.' We took another couple of sips from our glasses. The news had started and a bunch of politicians were mouthing away erratically. All they ever seemed to do was argue lately, so I got up and changed the channel to some music videos, still with no sound.

'What's Ana up to? I haven't seen her around lately.' Marko said.

'She's doing what I should be doing—preparing for school.'

'I don't know why she's so stressed. She could pass all her tests in her sleep.'

'Well, she does want to get into medical school, in Rijeka.' A short silence followed, as Marko seemed to think over what I had just said.

'What about you?' he finally said. 'You haven't even told me what your plans are after high school. They better involve me ...' he trailed off and smiled gently.

'Of course I'd tell you,' I said to him. 'It's just that I'm not even sure myself. But I was thinking perhaps ... Zagreb? They have a great faculty for science. I like the sound of biotechnology.'

'Zagreb, hey?' he said. More silence followed.

'So, yeah. What do you think?' I finally asked.

'Go for it, sounds great,' he said, somewhat unconvinced. I gave him a weak smile. I knew that Marko was a very fast learner and very practical, just not the 'book smarts' kind of guy. He had once loosely hinted at joining the local marine school and becoming a sailor, but I knew he was only considering it because that's what so many guys here ended up doing. It wasn't his passion though. Marko was good at many things, but not really *great* at anything in particular.

'What about you?' I asked tentatively. 'Thinking of earning some money?'

'Yeah, you know how it is now,' he said. 'We're entering a new age. Capitalism is coming, and I want to get on board. You don't need a university degree these days—you just need to get into business. Start making money and move on up, you know?'

In my mind, I groaned to myself. Marko had no idea what he was talking about. He had a habit of repeating things he heard other people say, as long as they sounded smart. He knew *nothing* about business but liked to talk about it as though he did. I knew he envisaged himself in the future as some sort of successful and wealthy man who wore a sharp navy-blue suit and worked for a flashy company in a fancy high-rise office building. Getting to that point, however, was no clear path. I chose not to say this though, despite how close we were.

'Yeah, you're totally right,' I told him. 'You could go far, Marko. Just get your foot in the door and you'll be the boss in no time!'

'Yeah, exactly!' he said, a little more enthusiastically now that he had my approval. 'I've done enough studying for this lifetime. Now I need some *life experience*.'

Another phrase he had heard from somewhere and repeated, despite not knowing what it meant.

'You'll be fine,' I said. 'I'll come and visit all the time from Zagreb and you can take me out for drinks every night, seeing as you'll be loaded with cash.'

He laughed at this and smiled at the thought, and I said nothing so as not to ruin the moment. I hoped for his sake that all of Marko's dreams would miraculously come true, and that he would find his way in life. I hoped we would stay friends, always able to sit around in silence, with only each other as company. We did just that for the remainder of the evening, until it got dark and Marko went back home. We never did go out that night.

Chapter 12

The beginning of not only a new year, but a new decade, was just hours away. Sometimes I loved thinking about how numbers worked, especially if they all fell into place conveniently. *1990.* The nineties; the end of high school for me and the beginning of university. A new decade, a new chapter in my life. I was the kind of person who always liked having a fresh start. I liked the sound of the next year, and I kept repeating it in my mind. *Nineteen, ninety ... nineteen ninety.*

'You're so weird,' Marko said to me. 'You wouldn't be so excited if it was 1991 or 1989 again. It's like every time you turn up the volume on the radio, it has to land on a multiple of ten. You and your numbers. Typical daughter of an army officer! You're so ... regimented.'

'Wow, Marko. Big word for such a small brain,' I teased.

He motioned to hit me playfully but pulled back at the last second. Marko then reached towards a small package on the side table and handed it to me. I was still putting my shoes on and saw it when I looked up. 'What's this?' I asked him.

'A little something for the New Year. I know we don't usually do presents, but hey. A new decade is pretty special.'

I blushed a little and couldn't help but smile. He had wrapped the gift so delicately, even placing a bow on top. I carefully peeled off the paper, glancing up at Marko whilst doing so. He was smiling in anticipation.

It was a book; *The Master and Margarita*, by Mikhail Bulgakov.

'I think you'll like this one,' Marko said to me. 'It's different.'

'Marko, I know I will love it!' I replied. 'I have wanted to read this one for so long. How is it that you're so good at choosing great books, anyway?'

'I have hidden talents,' Marko said, winking at me. I was so humbled by his gift, I felt ashamed that I hadn't been as thoughtful.

'I will have to make it up to you, really,' I said to him.

'Forget it. Your company is enough pleasure!' Marko said, unable to keep a straight face. I hit him softly with my new book, scowling at his sarcasm. I knew he couldn't remain serious for too long.

'Come on, Mara. You're welcome. I'm glad you like the book, but you will have to forget it for now. We have a big night to prepare for.'

I placed my copy of *The Master and Margarita* back on the side table and put my jacket on, then followed Marko out of the door and into the early evening. All the while I was smiling to myself, grateful to have Marko in my life.

We walked together towards the local supermarket, ready to arm ourselves with supplies for the great party that would be New Year's Eve. I had a long list of drinks to purchase, but Marko decided that he would be in charge of that. So, I put myself in charge of the food, instead. I purchased lots of hearty *slanina* and *pršut*, to line the insides of our stomachs, keep us warm and help us keep our alcohol down better. And to us, cheese and olives were a party necessity, along with loaves of fresh bread. Then there were snacks such as the crunchy *Smoki* and those delicious salty sticks that were so moreish. Mama had been kind enough to prepare a large selection of desserts for us, from *krempite* to *baklava* and everything else in between.

Everyone's favourite friend, Aleksandar, had been the only one to succeed in convincing his parents to give up their house for the night. Without much negotiation, his parents let him have the place to himself for the New Year's party. They chose to stay with relatives in Split for a few days, which Aleksandar was thrilled about. And we were all just as happy, since it meant we would end up destroying his place instead of our own homes.

I finished shopping for supplies in a hurry and unloaded them all on Marko, because I had to get to Ana's place soon and get ready with her.

'That's ok, I'll carry everything!' Marko called out to me as I was walking out the door of the supermarket.

'Yes, I know you will!' I answered back, shooting him a sly grin. He narrowed his eyes at me, pretending to be angry, but couldn't stop himself from smiling. The boy with smiling eyes, whose face was kind.

I noticed that he was becoming more and more lenient with me. He was always volunteering to help me out with just about anything, and he kept finding more and more excuses for just the two of us to hang out. He had even gifted me a new *Azra* t-shirt recently, for no reason at all, which he had asked his cousin in Zagreb to buy. I found myself thinking about Marko the whole way to Ana's place, and I didn't even realise it when I had reached the door of her apartment. It wasn't exactly a short walk, either.

As Ana and I prepared for the night, I considered talking to her about Marko, but I was too embarrassed. I wasn't even sure of how I really felt about him anyway. Maybe I was reading too much into it? Nonetheless, I found myself working much harder than usual to apply my make-up just right, paying close attention to every detail of my outfit, and taking special care not to crease my freshly-ironed *Azra* t-shirt.

'Do you remember our first make-up collection?' Ana asked me.

'You mean my mum's old black eyeliner, that cheap red lipstick and pressed powder that was about two shades lighter than our skin tone?'

'Yes, that's it!' Ana laughed. I smiled at her, remembering the 'collection'. We were so proud of those meagre pieces of cosmetics we had accumulated. We kept it all in a small, purple cosmetics bag, which we always shared. She would bring it to school during one week, then it was my duty the next week. It was the same with anything we got. Mama once gave me a bottle of cheap perfume she bought but didn't like, and Ana and I milked that bottle for every drop it had, dividing it equally between the two of us. It did not matter that we smelled like rotting flowers; the point was how *elegant* we felt.

'I still can't get over the loss of those cosmetics,' I said to Ana.

'I know, me too! I wish I knew who had stolen them. I'm going to hate that thieving girl forever.'

'Or boy,' I replied. We both laughed and continued to speculate about who could have stolen our purple cosmetics bag, deciding that it was most likely Ms Karamarko, our geography teacher. She always slathered on far more make-up than was necessary; the evidence was clearly against her.

I couldn't help but wonder at some point deep into my discussion with Ana, about where we would both be months from now. As excited as I was about the new year, I realised that soon enough there would be no more hanging out with Ana. She and I were going to be in different cities, drowning under the weight of our academic obligations. I hoped we would both make friends, but secretly, I didn't want her to find someone better than me. *A replacement.* I felt a pang of fear at the thought of such a drastically different future, but I erased the thought from my mind as quick as it came.

'Let's get going,' I said to Ana. I was more than ready now to stop thinking, and I thought the quickest way to achieve that was by succumbing to the effects of some *rakija*.

We met up with Nikola and Marko just before arriving at Aleksandar's place. The four of us were in great spirits, and Marko in particular could not stop cracking jokes and hounding me with his stories.

'Marko won't leave you alone, you know that?' Ana said seriously but with a smile on her face. I nudged her with my elbow, dismissing her observation, but I had noticed it. Marko wouldn't leave my side, but maybe, *maybe*, I was the one who wouldn't leave his.

My make-up had long since worn off, with only a faint line of pink rouge left on my lips. My eyeliner had smeared somewhat, but no one was noticing. Despite the cold, we had all warmed up enough to be able to rid ourselves of our coats and jackets. Marko smiled upon seeing my Azra t-shirt revealed from under my denim jacket. It matched my black jeans particularly well, giving me the punk-rock look I was going for.

'I don't know anyone else who looks so good in jeans,' Marko said to me over the noise of the speakers. I began to laugh, remembering how I had thought the exact same thing about him, not so long ago.

'No one except for Bruce Springsteen, right?' I replied. He gave me a strange look, and I realised he didn't really see Springsteen in the same way I do.

'Yeah, I guess so,' Marko said. 'But the Boss isn't really my type.'

I laughed again, partly at Marko's confusion, partly at my own silly comment, and mostly because I was steadily getting more drunk. Marko smiled at me and took my hand, leading me into the centre of the living room, where the dancing was most fervent and the music most intoxicating.

'*Par Godina Za Nas*' was blasting on the stereo as we began what felt like our tenth round of drinks at Aleksandar's place. Marko and I were singing the song to each other as loud as we could. We increased our pitch with each line (*They say that we only have just a couple of years for us*), and reached the loudest possible volume with the chorus (*Love me in a way like you have never loved before*) until we had scratched up our throats and needed to soothe them with more drinks.

At some point someone had smashed a glass, and someone else

had spilled wine all over the living room sofa. I had a vague memory of Aleksandar draping himself with his bed sheets before running outside into the winter night, but I don't remember seeing him again after that. Ana was laughing wildly at tall Ante's terrible jokes, while Nikola was mixing cocktails for anyone who dared drink them. Little Ante was handing out firecrackers, which I was briefly concerned about seeing as we were indoors, but I quickly forgot such insignificant worries.

We were all having fun. We were all drinking. But regardless of the alcoholic influences, I felt myself drawn to my closest and oldest friend, and he to me. I knew what was coming, and I did nothing to stop it. As the clock counted down the end of the decade, *Azra's* song '*Marina*' played on the stereo and ushered us into the new year. Marko, with his smiling eyes and whose face was kind, turned to me and kissed me.

He did not let go until sometime into the beginning of 1990.

Chapter 13

Twenty days after we had heralded in the new year and a new decade, we watched on television the Slovenian and Croatian delegates leave congress. There were big disagreements occurring in our nation's government, and it was a sign of things to come. I was not too concerned about anything, as per my usual self, but my Baka Roza was constantly making Nostradamus-like predictions for the future. I was not aware at the time, though, that what I interpreted as the semi-senile ravings of a war-damaged old woman were, in fact, accurate descriptions of what was awaiting us all.

'No, no, no, this is not good. This will be World War Two all over again!' Baka Roza announced. I grabbed the television remote and changed the channel, brightening up as the music of *EKV* came on, 'A Couple of Years for Us' dominating the screen. The song reminded me of the new year and I smiled, but perhaps it too was predicting what was soon to happen.

'No more news, Baka,' I said. 'It's damaging your mental health.'

'My mental health is as sharp as it ever was!' Baka Roza exclaimed. She shot me a look that reminded me to watch my attitude, but quite frankly, I was losing patience for her constant apocalyptic outbursts. I tried to tune out and focus on the music, but my wonderings about when I might get to see *EKV* perform live were disrupted once more by my grandmother.

'Mileva,' she said, taking me by surprise. I had almost forgotten the sound of my own name. 'You must believe me. This hysteria is exactly what let the evil-doers attract support during those terrible years many decades ago, and I can see history repeating itself, *Bože sačuvaj*. You are not worried because you are young and ignorant, but there are a lot of stupid and angry people out there. This is how it starts! They stop talking about *we*, and it becomes *us* and *them*. They change a few street names, no more of that *Partizan* history to remind us of our unity. Then, of course, they start blaming everyone but themselves. Now, all of a sudden, it is important where you're from—'

'I'm from Yugoslavia. We all are. End of story,' I interrupted her, attempting to end the conversation.

'No!' She yelled. I shut up, taken aback by her fiery disposition. 'It matters not where you were born. What matters is where your parents are from, where your grandparents are from, what they believe in and what their names are! Your identity is made up of everyone and everything before you, and the worst part is, you cannot change that even if you wanted to. Don't you understand? You are no longer a Yugoslav. You are a *Serb*, and you are living in *Croatia*. That is the problem.'

I had started listening by this point, and not out of pity. That was the first time I had ever been called a Serb. I had never really been made to consider my identity before, especially not my national identity. That was always something I could answer easily, and in one word: *Yugoslav*. But Baka Roza was complicating things for me. I mean, I knew that most of my family was of an Orthodox background, but since we did not grow up in a religious household, it did not really shape my identity. If anything, I felt more Dalmatian. I spoke the Croatian dialect, I lived and travelled almost entirely in this state of the country—it did not feel right to be called *anything* in particular, really.

'Mara,' my grandmother continued, more softly now. 'Listen to me. You need to be careful now, because to be who you are, where you are, is not going to be very popular. I think it will only get worse. I have seen people do terrible things ... and I have seen this state do terrible things before to its own brothers and sisters—to Serbs, to Jews, to Muslims, to Gypsies. There are right-wing tendencies within this part of our country. They were always there, and it looks like they've returned. Oh, I said this would happen the moment Tito died ...' she trailed off, looking worried and fearful.

I remembered Baka Roza's anxieties erupting back when our President died. A mild hysteria had consumed her and eventually faded away, but even then she had a dim prognosis for our country's future. I thought to myself, if Baka Roza turned out to be correct, then I would really have to buy her some sort of gift. Perhaps a crystal ball, not that she needed one.

We had gone to visit Marko's grandmother, who lived on the island *Pašman* across the sea from Zadar. I had taken the ferry there with Marko and his parents, braving the wind that blew across the water and slapped at my skin. Marko's grandmother was a funny old woman, one I couldn't quite figure out. She had her heart-warming moments, but she was also ruthless at times. On one occasion when we were younger, Marko had been left at home alone with his grandmother while his parents were out of town. He and I were playing in the courtyard like all the children, but when Marko didn't come inside on time when his grandmother had asked him to, she refused to let him back into the apartment until two in the morning. Marko maintains it was only because of his shouting and pounding on the door, angering the neighbours enough to complain, that his grandmother let him back inside.

When he told me the story, I asked whether that sort of treatment could be considered child abuse.

'Probably,' Marko said, shrugging indifferently. I didn't think it was the worst of the punishments he received growing up.

I was sitting in the bedroom in Marko's grandmother's house, reading a dated copy of the comic book, *Zagor*. The issue was called *Dangerous Waters* and it was one I had read before. I was too involved in the comic to notice what anyone else was doing.

'*Dangerous Waters?* Sounds like a comic book describing this country,' Marko's father said out loud, startling me. He was standing in the doorway. He hadn't meant it as a joke.

'Things are going to get dangerous around here, soon enough,' he said. I didn't know how to respond to this. Marko's father always had this strange ability to make me feel uncomfortable. It didn't help that he only ever spoke in statements to me, as though he were talking only to himself.

'Yeah ... you're probably right,' was all I could say in return. He held my gaze for a while as though trying to see through me, until I turned my eyes back onto the pictures of *Zagor*. I could still feel him standing in the doorway.

'I am right. You will see. All of you will see,' Marko's father said. And with that comment he turned away and left me to my thoughts. Who was he talking about? Me? What was I going to *see*? I had just been warned about something, but at that moment Marko walked into the room and disturbed my concentration.

'Marko, your dad just said the weirdest—'

'Ugh,' he groaned, not hearing me at all. 'Every time I'm here she makes me do some damn housework or maintenance around her giant property. She asked me to help her for a second and I ended up pulling weeds out of the footpath!' I brushed aside Marko's father's comments and instead laughed at Marko's plight, finding it amusing to see him so bitter.

'You're such a good grandson, what can I say?' I said to him. He grabbed a cushion off the sofa bed and hit me with it, knocking the comic book from my hands.

'Marko!' his grandmother yelled from the kitchen. 'Lunch is

ready! You two come and eat now!'

'We're not hungry!' Marko replied.

'Don't be stupid! Eat now before the food gets cold!'

'No, we'll eat later!'

'It will be cold!'

'Well, I'll just heat it up again!'

'What? And waste my electricity? I don't think so!'

'Then we'll starve!'

'Good!'

Marko let out a sigh, swearing under his breath. 'Can you feel the love?' he asked me, rolling his eyes towards the kitchen.

A few moments later, we heard his grandmother's voice again. 'Marko! Lunch is on the table!' I interrupted Marko just as he was about to yell back to his grandmother.

'Let's just eat,' I told him, knowing it was the only way towards a peaceful solution. So we went into the kitchen and sat down to eat the barbecued fish, silverbeet and potato salad. This kind of Dalmatian food was so light that it would hardly fill us up anyway, and we would only be hungry again within an hour or so.

Marko's father was swearing loudly at some politician on the screen, claiming that none of them had any idea what they were doing, and they could all go to hell. Marko kept glancing up at me while we ate, and I knew he felt ashamed by his father's behaviour and crudeness. I wasn't really fazed by it, but I felt bad knowing Marko was embarrassed. I didn't want him to feel like that. I wanted him to know that I had no problem with his family, because they were his, so I loved them all the same.

The stay at Marko's grandmother's house was only short, and I was glad I did not have to spend more than one night there. I usually had no problem being around his family, even with their quirks, but lately I was growing tired of Marko's father and his political rants. This wasn't helped by the silence of Marko's mother, who was usually the best source of conversation, nor by Marko's awkward self-consciousness. On the ferry ride back to Zadar I managed to block out any discussion (which was lucky considering Marko's father had gotten into a heated talk with another man on the ferry). Both of them were firing away at everyone and everything, criticising every last aspect of Yugoslavia and its inhabitants.

When we arrived in the city, I began to take notice of the posters and graffiti appearing, all of which was politically motivated. People were beginning to take sides; either a united Yugoslavia or a divided one. It was seeping through the pores of the city and breaking out, like one of the many weeds that Marko had to tear out from his grandmother's yard. The toxic discussion was everywhere; in cafés, grocery stores and workplaces, and more than anywhere, on the television.

But at that point I wasn't worried. I was quietly observant, but nothing more.

I watched on with a vague sense of interest, but no deeper sense of worry. That's not to say I wasn't distracted; rather, I had *one* predominant distraction in my life. The changing political landscape was no competition for Marko, who had become highly successful at consuming my every waking thought. At times I had to remind myself that I was but a short while away from graduating high school, presuming I passed all my exams, of course. I needed to leave some space in my brain for all the numbers and dates I had to memorise, which meant pushing Marko to the back of my mind.

But not all the way back.

Ana was amused by the slight changes in my behaviour, but ultimately she was happy for me. But Nikola had become noticeably indifferent towards Marko's and my relationship, and to just about anything else regarding our social lives.

It was Easter time, and I noticed more people than ever celebrating. My family, as predicted, did not mark the event. Either way, the Catholic Easter seemed to take precedent. Marko had invited me over to celebrate with his family, but somehow, I managed to come up with an excuse. It felt like everyone was busy doing something for Easter, bar a few of us. I spent the holiday with Nikola instead, helping each other revise for our upcoming exams.

Neither of us mentioned Easter at all.

Had the timing been different, had things with Marko happened earlier or later, then perhaps I might have been enlightened enough to notice what Nikola was noticing. Alas, my distraction in the form of Marko had blinded me to all that was occurring, right when I needed to open my eyes more than ever before.

And Marko was not like me. Marko fitted right in. Marko saw nothing to worry about, nothing wrong with whatever was happening or with what was going to happen. So, I thought likewise. I felt safe.

I loved Marko, and he loved me.

But I suppose we never got around to having that one conversation we should have had. I glided through life on the basis of so many presumptions; presumptions about my country, about Marko and about myself. In my world, everything always met my expectations. My country would find a way to carry on, unharmed, and Marko would always be the accepting and loving person I thought he was. He would step up and prove himself to be intelligent, thus proving wrong all those who doubted him.

Graduation day was full of mixed emotions. More than anything we were all relieved to have successfully completed school. Many of us felt excited about what was to come next. But there was also sadness from the realisation that our group of friends would no longer be seeing each other almost every day. As stressful as our final year of high school had been, it had also been comforting to have had each other and to have been within the familiar confines of our school.

Marko came along to our graduation as a guest, having already had his own just days before. He had managed to complete high school after all, and actually performed quite well. Yet it was not enough to please his father, who didn't see the need to take any photos or celebrate in any way on the day of Marko's graduation.

To absolutely no one's surprise, Nikola had finished with the best results in the entire school. He finished top in the region, too, and was sitting comfortably knowing he would most definitely get into the university he wanted. Ana also did exceptionally well but still had to go through the same application process for medical school as all others who were interested. I was more fortunate because getting into my chosen degree would not be so complicated. I knew I had gotten good enough results to get me through.

Thinking back, it was so stupid, really. It didn't make sense that so much weighting was put onto this one small time of our lives; onto a few final tests and exams which gave but a fraction of indication towards how well we had learned and understood our subjects. Surely there was more to life than end of year high school results. Surely as people we would be defined by so much more than just our careers.

We held the after-party at tall Ante's place. Our whole graduating class was there, including other students from other schools, and the usual few who liked to cling on. I was in good spirits, but I was holding back, too. I wasn't the same uninhibited person from previous parties. I was looking at everyone and considering their loyalties: *Serb or Croatian; Catholic or Orthodox*. Why should it even matter? The more I considered it, the more I felt like an outsider.

Nikola came up to me and took my hand, pulling me away into a corridor. While most people were outside socialising, he and I stood in this dimly lit, narrow space, facing each other.

'Hey, what's going on?' I asked him. Nikola looked at me and pulled something out of the inside pocket of his jacket. At first, I couldn't quite understand what it was, but then I noticed it was two painted hard-boiled eggs. I let out a laugh.

'What's this? What on earth are you carrying eggs around for?'

'I know it looks stupid,' Nikola replied, 'but there's a reason,' he said, a little more seriously now. He handed me an egg and showed me how to hold it between my two hands. He held the other egg the same way.

'Ok, now you have to make a wish,' Nikola said to me.

'Are we cracking eggs?' I asked, still confused.

'Yes, obviously, so just do it.'

I obliged and thought about a wish. There were so many things I could wish for myself, but when I looked up at Nikola and studied the expression on my friend's face, I knew straight away what I wanted.

'Ready?' he asked. I nodded. Nikola motioned for me to crack my egg on top of his, and I did so. There was a crack in his egg, but not mine. We swapped roles, and he cracked his egg onto mine. This time he won.

'Ok, one more time, on the side,' he announced. We turned our painted eggs over and had another go. My egg put a crack in his, and I won.

'Well, there you go,' Nikola said, smiling. I looked back at him, still wondering why we were doing this.

'We belong too, Mara. We have our traditions as well, and even though we don't get to show it, I'll be damned if they're going to stop us from being who we are.'

I looked back at him with determination and unexpectedly felt hot tears in the corners of my eyes.

'Sorry for being so late—I know Orthodox Easter passed a couple of months ago,' Nikola said, laughing a little.

'That's ok, it's never too late,' I replied.

'And you know,' he went on, 'It's not even about Easter. It's not about those silly traditions, or whatever else—'

'I know,' I interrupted him. 'It's about who we are, and our right to be here. Our right to exist freely.'

Nikola nodded, looking at me and seeing right into my heart. Only he could feel what I was feeling at that very moment.

We hugged each other and held on for a while. Then we finally decided to eat the eggs, laughing at the whole situation. I hoped that my wish really would come true. I wished for Nikola to have a happy life.

Chapter 14

I watched Mama nervously chain-smoke through a pack of Marlboro Reds. A sinking feeling of guilt was creeping up on me, and I felt helpless and frustrated. I knew my mother would struggle enough just having to watch me leave for another city, but the circumstances made it all the more difficult.

As I walked out into the courtyard, I took one last glance up towards my mother who was leaning on the balcony door. The smoke of her cigarette was clouding her face, but it was not enough to conceal the tears that filled her eyes and spilled onto her cheeks.

I didn't look back as my father drove the car away towards the *kolodvor*. Alisa was silent in the backseat. Mama had been painfully quiet these last few months, swallowing her emotions so much that she barely felt the need to eat anything. I worried that I had neglected Alisa, too, in my mad focus to finish school and get out of Zadar. She was quiet and I wondered what her young mind was thinking. My eyes met Alisa's in the rear-view mirror and she held my gaze but didn't smile. She was 12 years old and I wondered if she was becoming a sulky teenager. But I knew that wasn't the real reason.

I looked ahead as we approached the bus station. Marko was there, waiting to see me off. He helped me take my things out of the car and load them onto the bus that was waiting. The bus driver stood by the door and watched us, with one arm leaning up against the bus, exposing the dark patches of sweat in his armpits. He had a cigarette in his mouth, and I wondered how anyone could possibly enjoy smoking in the sticky heat of summer, particularly next to an overheated bus that was emanating steam from the engine.

My father came to give me one last hug. 'I'll leave you and Marko to say your goodbyes,' he said. He turned to go back towards the car and for a moment I wanted to stop him. I didn't want him to leave me any earlier than he had to. Marko was saying something to me, but I wasn't really listening. I was wondering who I would miss the most.

'Mara, are you all right? Stop looking so sad. We'll be seeing each other in no time,' Marko said after I finally tuned in to him. I felt a pang of anger towards Marko. How could he remain so upbeat? But I allowed myself to soften and I gave him a huge hug (though, what I had really wanted to do was to slap him across the head).

I went and took my seat on the bus, somewhere towards the end but next to a window. And as the bus reversed out of its parking spot and onto the road ahead, I looked out at Marko with a strange feeling in my chest. Something didn't feel right, but I pushed the bad feeling aside and pretended everything was fine.

Autumn in Zagreb felt different in reality than in my mind. It was meant to be picturesque, bustling with students who were full of anticipation for the next year of their studies, moving one step closer to their chosen careers and their independence. It was not meant to feel so tense, so cold and so uncertain.

I had been mentally planning this special period for the past year of my life; moving out of Zadar, entering a new city and a new institution. In my mind, it was like something out of a movie. In my mind, it was going to be a time of self-discovery and fulfilment and attaining knowledge. Hours were to be spent perusing the dusty and majestic rows of the university library, learning from the great minds of those before me.

In reality, it felt like absolute horror.

I had been naïve for not taking into consideration the changes around me. I believed that the world would continue to function normally, if only to accommodate my transition into adulthood. Why was the world working against me, then?

I had deliberately found myself some cheap student accommodation away from the city centre and closer to the river Sava. I was desperate to avoid the hive that was the main square and its surroundings. I spent my last few days leading up to the start of the academic year in a bored haze, wandering the streets of Zagreb and watching the locals rhythmically going about their daily lives. But there was no way I could ignore the new flags appearing, and the old ones disappearing.

I called Marko from time to time, and I missed him. When I attempted to explain to him the atmosphere of the city, he told me to change my perspective.

'Look at it as a time of great change and excitement, Mara.'

'You don't understand, these changes aren't good,' I replied.

'Stop being so pessimistic ...'

We thought differently on the issue, so I never chose to pursue it. I thought to myself, if only Marko could be here, then he could see what I meant. But Marko was in Zadar, where the level of fanaticism was reaching fever pitch. I knew from the phone conversations with Mama that things in Zadar were no better; worse, in fact. He must have been blind not to notice it.

I didn't think for a moment, however, that Marko would be susceptible to any of it. When I chatted to Marko and listened to him try and cheer me up, I didn't think he really meant it. I didn't think he really ... *agreed* with what was being said. But I guess I refused to believe just how impressionable he could be.

I was trying my hardest to keep in touch with all my friends. I wrote to Ana frequently and called her when I could. She had made it into medical school in Rijeka without much difficulty, just as I knew she would. I joked with her that she was finally up north and closer to Italy, just as she had always dreamed, and could now go shopping in Trieste whenever she pleased. We laughed about it, although we knew it was just a light-hearted joke. 'I'll wait for you to visit before I go on any extravagant shopping trips,' she said to me one day over the phone. That was her way of telling me she missed me. And of telling me that she felt uncomfortable about what was happening.

Fortunately for Ana, things were a bit calmer in Istria. That part of the country always seemed to escape the extremism occurring elsewhere. People were just different there, more accepting, calmer and less judgemental. But I couldn't help but think that Ana was fortunate anyway, seeing as she was a Croatian and therefore had nothing to fear. Her family was living life as they always had. She was under no pressure to leave, and she made her life decisions purely on what was in her best interests.

Did I resent her for it? Was I envious of her safety, of her lack of concern? Most definitely. But I never revealed that shallow side of me, not to anyone.

Nikola was in a similar situation to me. But he was smart and calculating. He had decided a while ago to enrol into a university in Serbia. He chose to go to Novi Sad, where he had a lot of family on his mother's side. And his mother chose to go, too. They packed up everything in Zadar and moved to northern Serbia. He sounded positive.

'Mara, we are finally happy again,' he told me on the phone one afternoon. 'It wasn't easy, but we made the right choice. My mother has family here and they helped her find good work. We have a nice place to live and the city is beautiful.'

I was genuinely happy for him. No one had suffered so much like Nikola and there was no one more deserving of a happy and stable life.

'Mara, you must come and visit some time. The trip from Zagreb to Novi Sad is so short! Please, I can tell by your voice that you need some company.' Nikola was right, but I shrugged off his comments and told him not to worry.

'I'm actually pretty busy with university, but thanks,' I would respond, automatically.

I was glad that Nikola was safe and doing well. I was glad that Ana was enjoying her studies and her new city. It was Marko who worried me.

'They have changed the constitution,' my father told me.

'What? What do you mean?' I replied. I was on the phone to Tata, who was becoming increasingly anxious. There was a lot of serious discussion surrounding the impending shift from his usual desk job at work to a more 'hands-on' role.

'What I mean is they have adopted a new one. Some of our rights are no longer there.'

'Whose rights?' I asked.

'The rights of Serbs, Mara.'

I thought about what he was saying to me. So much for my effort to distance myself from politics. Here was my own father calling me with updates every second day, like an unwanted news report.

'Just be careful, ok?' he said, his voice less agitated.

'Tata, I think you're overreacting.'

'Hope for the best, prepare for the worst. Do you hear me?'

'Yes,' I sighed, rolling my eyes at the military expression so deeply ingrained in his mind.

'I wish you could be here for the holidays. But you obviously have a lot on your plate. Keep focusing on your studies, and please come and visit when you have some time to spare,' Tata said.

'Of course, I will, Tata,' I said.

I felt a bit guilty in telling my parents I wouldn't be coming back to Zadar for the winter break. It was true I had a lot of work to do, but not so much that it would inhibit me from taking a break. Despite the difficulty I had adjusting to Zagreb, I just didn't feel like returning to such a tense atmosphere back home. Not that long ago I would have given anything to return to Zadar, even for a short while. But now I felt like avoiding it. I was scared that things at home had changed too much.

And then I got to thinking … what kind of nation removes an entire group of people from its constitution? What did they have planned?

I contemplated the winter break alone and the likelihood of welcoming in the new year without my closest friends and family. I hesitated for a moment and almost told Tata that I would be coming back, but I just couldn't get the words out in time.

Although I remained in Zagreb through the winter break, I didn't end up spending it alone. Marko announced to me that he would come and see me, and I perked up at his thoughtfulness and at the prospect.

I greeted Marko at the bus station. He looked as handsome as ever. He was in great spirits and kept saying how happy he was to be in our 'nation's capital'. This irritated me, but I ignored it. I didn't want it to ruin our reunion.

We took the bus to my small one-bedroom apartment, chatting about anything and everything. Soon enough I began to relax and forgive myself of the worries that burdened my waking mind; allowing myself to just be with Marko. When he spoke to me, I found myself looking at him fondly, just as I had done so many times before.

My apartment was nothing special, nor was Marko expecting it to be. The walls were covered with faded floral-patterned wallpaper— capable of providing some warmth to an otherwise sterile space. I was fortunate enough to have central heating throughout the living room, even if the radiators only emitted a limited amount of heat. The apartment had come with much of the furniture already provided, including the sofa, television cabinet, wooden wardrobe and bed frame. Mama and Tata had given me enough money to purchase a mattress and some other bits and pieces, and I had managed to bring some bedding and towels from home. It was *liveable*.

Marko made himself comfortable on the sofa, which sunk under his weight. I brought out some food and offered drinks and we watched music videos on the small television set in the corner. Such times were the only moments that I can truly remember us as being perfectly harmonious; where nothing needed to be said but everything made perfect sense. There were no differences between us, no histories dragging us away and into opposing futures. Nothing before us mattered. All I cared about, right then and there, was this person before me who knew me so well and for whom my loyalty never wavered from.

Sometimes Marko would have this raw look in his eyes, if only for a fleeting second, as though to tell me that *this* was really him, in his most honest form. Sometimes, the look in his eyes was one seeking forgiveness, as though he was about to betray me.

But any betrayal that was to come was not from the same Marko.

The next morning, I awoke to the smell of coffee wafting into my nostrils. I opened my eyes only slightly to see Marko hovering over me with a coffee cup in his hand, gently blowing over it so that the scent enveloped my face. I smiled at him sleepily and laughed, and he placed the coffee on the bedside table. I sat up, wondering what time it was.

'Here's breakfast,' Marko said, taking the coffee and putting it into my hands. 'I went to the bakery while you were still asleep and got us some savoury rolls.'

'When did you wake up?'

'Before you.'

'Oh, you don't say.'

We sat together, keeping close for warmth whilst drinking the coffee and eating the savoury rolls. In the unforgiving light beaming

122

through the windows, I felt slightly self-conscious, knowing that I couldn't have been a very flattering image first thing in the morning. But Marko gave no indication of seeing me in an unattractive light. He seemed incredibly content, and I used the time to focus instead on him and on how the sunshine glinted on the golden hairs across his jawline, or the way his muscles had become more defined, his chest more pronounced.

All the work he had been doing since school finished had been manual labour, so it wasn't surprising to see his body had become well-formed and fuller. I, on the other hand, had probably wasted away into a listless form, if my body was at all a reflection of my mood. But all that negativity appeared to have left me now that Marko was here. I was sorry that he could not stay for but a few days, but it was enough. He and I were okay; we were going to be okay.

Once Marko had returned to Zadar, I tried hard to find a way to cope in Zagreb. I surrounded myself with only positive people and pushed myself academically. Only every so often would I venture into the density of the city centre and expose myself to the changing world. I was, however, beginning to lose my sense of optimism. It did not take long after Marko's departure for me to be reminded of the forces of change that were taking over society.

At the beginning of May, anti-Yugoslav rioters systemically targeted Serbian businesses in Zadar, smashing windows, stealing and vandalising properties. Their actions appeared to go unpunished, Mama relayed to me over the phone. It was Zadar's *Kristallnacht*. Baka Roza was so panicked that she made my mother and sister stay at a friend's apartment that evening, out of fear that Serbs would be targeted in their homes. From the friend's balcony, Alisa watched her neighbours, the people of her town, use clubs to smash the windows of Serbian-owned kiosks, taking what they could and setting the remains alight.

And I was supposed to go back to this city I called home.

Chapter 15

I would never forget my father's blue eyes that appeared to harbour the world. Sheltered beneath his heavy brow, his eyes glittered with a certain wisdom that only he possessed. His eyes were as warm as his arms were giant, which felt like blankets when wrapped around me. In his arms was where I felt safest. Standing next to him was where I felt proudest; beside the man that was larger than life, watching all those around him. *Incomparable.*

Men would stare and shake his hand in adoration, and they would always use both hands, as though attempting to fully grasp the enormity of the man and whatever it was that made him so great. My father would use only his right hand, fully outstretched to ensure some distance, as though to distinguish himself from the others.

Women, however, would shamelessly flirt with him, falling for his charms like dominoes. They would look down at me, considerably shorter and smaller than my father in every sense. 'So *you're* his daughter,' they would say with eyes wide open, astonished almost, at the sight of me. I would smile, flattered to be associated with such a man, to be recognised as his daughter. It was his blood that flowed through my veins. My eyes, dark as night, didn't reflect his starlit eyes, the colour of the ocean. My meek brown hair was nothing in comparison to his starkly rich, dark hair. He was tall; I was short. He was handsome; I was plain. Yet we never left each other's sides.

On the 25th of June, Slovenia declared independence. Croatia was soon to follow. While many were panicking about what was going to become of our country, and others were celebrating the newfound 'freedom', I could only think of what was going to become of my father. As an army man, he had a job to do now.

For the first time since the trouble had started, I was terrified.

I was prepared for the journey that awaited my father. He had to do his service and there was no question about that. It was the news that Marko fed me, of his own service, that I wasn't prepared for, and which really brought my world crashing down.

I wanted nothing more upon my return to Zadar, after a year of study, than to be back with Marko—back to our old relationship. I felt that if I could at least have that, then everything else would seem insignificant.

I underestimated how much a person could change in just one year. Especially someone as painfully clueless as Marko. I had always been glad he paid no attention to politics, for it sheltered him. Instead, his lack of opinion had left an open void—one that had since become filled with a nationalist agenda.

I remembered the saying, 'If you don't stand for something, you will fall for anything.'

I didn't come back to find the melancholic, indifferent Marko of a year ago; the Marko who managed to flow through life almost effortlessly. He wasn't the same companion who would take me out to rock concerts, watch basketball matches with me and go walking along the *Riva* just to pass the time. He had become consumed by other ideas, and I felt his new persona emanating from his body, like a strange presence had taken over him.

When he came to greet me at the bus station, I jumped straight into his arms. He hugged me tightly as usual, but his breath felt heavy on my neck. It didn't feel right.

'It's good to see you,' Marko said. 'Come on, let's get you back home.' I nodded, and we set off. He placed my luggage into the back of his father's car and proceeded to drive us to our familiar address.

'How's work?' I asked, feeling stupid. That's the sort of question you ask a neighbour passing by, or an acquaintance; not one's partner, after not having seen them in months. But it was all I could think to say.

'It was going well, but there has been a change of plans,' Marko said.

I wondered if this was his sugar-coated way of saying he got fired.

'Ugh, it's hot in here. Can you roll your window down?' he continued.

I wouldn't really care if he had lost his job or even if he had to move. These were all little hiccups and we'd get over them. But I did realise he had obviously made a choice already and hadn't bothered to let me know. That was disappointing.

'Well?' I pressed. 'What's the change of plans? Whatever it is, I'm sure it will work out.'

Marko kept his eyes defiantly on the road before him.

'Mara,' he finally said. 'I've joined the army. I wanted to tell you, but I didn't know how. So I just had to say it. I've got a new job now, defending the country.'

I wished he had been fired. That would have been bearable news.

'What the hell did you just say?' I asked.

'The army. You know, they—'

'I know exactly what the army is. Where do you think my father has been working all his life!'

And then the worst part hit me.

'Wait a second, Marko. Whose army?'

'Well, our country's,' he said, with obvious caution in his voice.

'And what country would that be?' I asked, my voice now

considerably quieter.

'Croatia, of course.'

I was completely floored. I looked at Marko, attempting to communicate everything I was thinking by the expression on my face. Joining the army—in my opinion, a risky thing to do. Joining the army on the verge of war—a suicidal thing to do. Joining the army of our 'new' country?

'Marko … you do know what my father does, right?' I said.

'Yes, I know …' Marko said uncomfortably.

'For the… Yugoslav Army,' I said.

'Yes, I know …' Marko said once more. All emotion had left his voice.

' I…' I stuttered. I was at a loss.

I didn't bother asking why he had chosen to do this, if he would reconsider, or whether there was any sense of rational thought operating in his mind anymore. I hoped to hell that the political turmoil would be just that: politics and change, and that war would be averted. I didn't think I could handle anything more.

Marko let out a heavy sigh and mumbled something. It sounded like 'sorry', but I didn't care. That was just an empty word.

I looked out the window and let the breeze whip around my face and flick away the tears that had stuck to my eyes. The mountains of Velebit, once projecting imagery of boundless opportunities and high hopes, now looked more like a barrier. They were trapping me in the town that was once my sanctuary but had now become a prison.

And Marko … he had become the prison guard.

I did not know what to say to myself, let alone to others. I couldn't tell Nikola and Ana. How could I reveal Marko's betrayal to anyone? But while I was engrossed in my internal grief, our city was discarding us. Serbs were a blemish on the beautiful face of Croatia, and Dalmatia was a hotbed for hatred.

The summer was deepening as emotions were rising, and I felt I finally had to confide in my mother. I could no longer feign politeness and I had to tell her about Marko's choice and how deeply it had cut me. But every time I gained the strength to speak up, I faltered. And then one day she said something to confuse me even further.

'Mara, I don't think you should return to Zagreb in the springtime.' Mama said to me. It didn't sound like a request, but more like a demand. 'In fact, I don't think you should stay in Zadar either.'

'Well … where should I go? Where could I possibly go if I can't be here with you?' I asked.

'Zadar is too dangerous for you.' she started.

'Isn't it too dangerous for all of us?' I responded, maybe a little defensively.

'Yes, it is. But so long as your father is still here, I'm not leaving. And I still have a job and a role to keep food on the table and a roof over our heads. And Alisa … she is still a child. She needs routine, she needs to go to school. But you are an adult, and you are on your own in Zagreb. And you cannot afford to be alone right now.'

It was as though Mama could read my mind all along.

'And I don't think you can rely on Marko, to be perfectly honest.' she said.

Mama looked almost angry when she said this.

'I want to stay with you …' I spluttered. I did not feel like an adult in this moment. I wanted Mama. I wanted Tata home.

'I will feel better, knowing you are somewhere safer, but with family.' Mama powered on, clenching her jaw. 'Just for a while. Just until this is over.'

My head was spinning and I didn't know how much more change I could handle. But looking at Mama, I could see her heart in her throat.

'I will do whatever you think is best. Just don't be sad, *Mama moja*.' And I hugged her, like a child.

My mother's difficult decision to practically deport me to my uncle's place in Sarajevo was made with her best intentions in mind. I believe it was the first time for as long as I could recall that my education was no longer my parent's number one priority. My degree was to be put on the backburner. Zagreb was stirring. Zadar was stirring. Sarajevo was the centre of Yugoslavia and would be the last place for violence to erupt. It was the bedrock of *brotherhood and unity*.

And at least it was *a little bit* closer to home than Belgrade. I liked that.

Yet something within me didn't sit right. I suppose it was a sense of powerlessness I felt. And maybe, finally and rightfully; anger.

I had reached a point in my life where I felt enticed by a sense of exhilarating recklessness. With nothing around me going according to plan, I barely reacted to the news of having to be uprooted from my surroundings in order to spend the foreseeable future in Bosnia's capital. No more studying? No more routine? Why the hell not. I was compelled by a sense of bitterness, which was accompanied by my lust for the unknown and was brought on by my disappointment towards everyone and everything around me. My parents were on the verge of hysteria and Marko had devastated me. No one seemed to talk about the future anymore, unless it was to do with their fear of it.

Screw them, was all I could think.

Out of spite, I acted as though everything was going exactly as I had wanted. I *wanted* to leave, and to leave them behind. They were the ones who decided to let me go first, after all, and all my childish mind could think was, *they started it! Not me!*

In reality, I was being a coward. My own mother and younger sister were to stay in Zadar and bear the brunt of the fear and isolation. They would 'hold down the fort', so to speak, while I was running away like a child to the safety of her bed, hiding beneath the covers. Ignoring the situation wouldn't make it go away, and the bitterness that consumed me didn't help to mend my relationship with Marko.

Before the summer ended, I made one last trip to Lika. I do not know why I considered it a 'last trip', but it sure felt like it. It reminded me of those summers long ago, when I could hardly wait to run into the safe arms of Baka and Dida. I did the same this time round, surprising Dida Ilija, who had not been able to catch me in his arms for several years now. I held onto him longer than usual. He didn't let go of me for a while either.

The atmosphere in Lika had also changed. Baka and Dida informed me that many people had packed up and left. Most of the elderly people still stayed though, and Baka told me she had no reason to be fearful of anything. She still believed common sense and goodness would prevail, and no real harm could come to innocent civilians.

The house in Lika had been missing something ever since Ninja passed away. Baka and Dida never saw him die, but they noticed him walking off one day and he never returned. Dida explained to me that dogs do that when they know they are going to die; they go and find a cool, secluded place and lie there, ready to let life leave them.

But now, with no dog and only a few chickens in the yard, my grandparents' home felt eerily quiet. The slow exodus of the local population also meant that less neighbours came by to visit, and I think this also had a depressing effect on Baka and Dida.

'Don't worry about us,' Baka kept reassuring me. 'We will be fine here. But it is smart of you to leave this place and go east. Even if the tension doesn't amount to anything here, it will still be safer somewhere else.'

I looked at my grandmother and nodded quietly, then looked back down at the chess board before me. I was playing with Dida and it was my turn. I had been deliberating for a minute now and still didn't know how to make my move. Despite all the practice and education he gave me, Dida still defeated me at chess every time. I liked that he wasn't soft on me. He criticised me for being out of practice and I laughed, telling him he was absolutely right. I was indeed out of practice.

I made my move and Dida saw the gap I had left and went straight for my knight. *Damn.* That was a painful loss.

'Sometimes, Mara, it is hard to predict what the right move will be,' Dida said. 'You can plan all you like, you can put all the structures in place, have all the right thinking, alas ... when things take a turn for the worst, you find yourself abandoning all logic and simply looking for small victories, playing move-by-move and forgetting the big picture.' I knew he was talking about more than this game of chess.

I looked back at him and gently shook my head, wishing he could see into my mind and understand all the million thoughts ricocheting off each other. It was all so simple for Dida. For him, life itself could make perfect sense just by arranging one's mind and one's thought processes in the right way. Dida was not a complicated man. He sought no greater power, no control over others. There were so few men like him, especially now and especially in this land of ours.

Dida reached over and took my hand in his, and I smiled back at him. He *did* understand the barrage of thoughts that attacked my mind. It was my turn once more to make a move on the chessboard and I thought ahead. I saw an opportunity to claim Dida's bishop and after weighing up the potential risks, I went for it. My own bishop claimed his and was left in the clear with no way of being attacked.

'That's better,' Dida gave me a wink.

Saying goodbye to Baka and Dida was difficult. We all tried to treat it like any other time I was returning home, but of course it was impossible to ignore the unspoken fears we all had. I managed to bid them farewell without any obvious emotional turmoil, but Baka couldn't help but shed a few tears. I could hardly look at Dida, and the one time I did make eye-contact with him was enough to put a knot in my throat. I had to look away, and I moved towards my car even quicker.

I drove away with the image of my grandparents in the rear-view mirror growing smaller and smaller. Tata was already on call 24/7 and unable to leave the barracks. I didn't even get to see him. I gripped the steering wheel hard, knowing his hands had held it too, not so long ago. I only had a couple of days left before my bus ride to Sarajevo. I decided to make one more stop before I returned to Zadar.

I headed along the coastline towards the *selo*, knowing that at this point most of the holidaying tourists would have returned back to their usual busy lives and be awaiting the arrival of autumn. I drove slowly, even making a few stops on the way. I wanted to pay close attention to this part of the country and to have every stone, every hillside and every small inlet of sea imprinted into my long-term memory. I wanted so badly to remember it all, so that if I were ever asked to paint a picture of this landscape, I could recreate every square metre of it with perfect precision and do justice to the sheer beauty of this part of the world.

After a few short hours I pulled up into the driveway of Uncle Dmitar's home, assuming he would be surprised to see me. It was as quiet as I expected it to be, and even more so as the afternoon was dwindling and a pink hue took over the skyline. I strolled around the house and towards the front veranda, and from there I could see Dmitar sitting on the concrete jetty, eating oysters.

He noticed my presence and looked up, then smiled when he realised who I was. I walked over and sat next to him, but not too close to the oysters. I never had been a fan of shellfish, despite quite liking most other seafood. It made me a very rare breed of Dalmatian.

'Here, your favourite,' Dmitar said to me jokingly, handing me a freshly shucked oyster. Eating oysters straight from the sea, with a squeeze of fresh lemon cutting through the saltiness of the Adriatic, gave it a fairy-tale like feeling. I had watched my family swallow fresh oysters whole with absolute delight, but the moment I looked at oysters the fairy-tale ended. I declined any invitation to eat the oyster and pushed my uncle's hand, and the oyster, back to him with a grin.

'Who knows when you'll have another opportunity to eat seafood as fresh as this,' Dmitar said.

I wanted to make some offhand comment to indicate how that didn't bother me at all, but I didn't believe Dmitar would buy my act. Sitting there in that spot in the *selo*, watching the sun set, and hearing nothing but the sea water sloshing against the jetty and the scraping of Dmitar's knife against oyster shells, I began to feel differently about leaving my home.

'What am I doing?' I said aloud without really meaning to. I wasn't looking at Dmitar, but out to sea, where the islands looked like silhouettes against the backdrop of the setting sun.

'You're doing what any person with a hint of sense in them would do. You're getting the hell out of here,' Dmitar said. 'If you were *really* smart, you'd leave this whole country entirely, go as far away as possible. Australia, New Zealand perhaps.'

'Then why are you staying?' I asked. I couldn't help but notice that all the people telling me to leave weren't going anywhere themselves.

'I'm old,' replied Dmitar. 'What's the use? There's nowhere for me to start again, nor is there a point in starting again.'

I nodded, realising what he meant.

'And besides.' he continued, 'there's no way in hell I'm letting those bastards force me out of my own damn home.'

I laughed out loud at this and Dmitar couldn't help but chuckle as well. I smiled at his stubbornness, and at how much Dmitar was like his sister. Yet on the other hand, he wasn't exactly being stubborn. He was fighting for his place, for his right to remain an inhabitant of the *selo*. This was his identity and no one could tell him otherwise.

'I should be doing the same though, shouldn't I?' I asked my great uncle. 'You're right. This is *our* home. By leaving, I'm just reaffirming what they want us to believe: that we don't belong here.'

'You are both right and wrong,' Dmitar responded. 'You're right in saying that this is our land, and that for them, seeing us leave is a victory. But you're wrong in saying that you should be doing the same as some others by staying here out of principle … because if you don't leave on your own terms, then they will find other ways to get rid of you. And you are too young and have too bright a future to take that risk and to resign yourself to the life of a second-class citizen in your own home.'

I remained in the *selo* with Dmitar that night, sleeping in the same room where I had spent just about every summer of my life so far. A cool shift had come with the night, and I had to grab an extra blanket from the cupboard. To my amazement, I fell asleep quite effortlessly. In my dreams I could feel myself rocking as though on a boat out at sea, and although it felt rough at first, the motions soon slowed and became soothing, almost calming, until I felt like I was floating along in the right direction.

Chapter 16

I told Marko he didn't need to be there to see me off. I told him it would be too emotional, and that I didn't want him to think of my departure as permanent. Marko did not take the news well and thought that it was unnecessary for me to leave Croatia at all. I was trying terribly hard to overcome the anger I had been feeling towards him. I wanted to maintain some peace between us, and to understand where he was coming from. But I couldn't see beyond the hurt.

'What's the difference?' I said to him after he'd once again argued against my move to Sarajevo. 'It's not like you'll be here to keep me company anyway. Who knows where they'll send you.' I was displaying my bitterness towards Marko now, making no effort to hide my disdain towards militarism all together.

'I don't know for sure where I'll end up, but I still want you to be here. I do plan to return, you know,' Marko had said.

'Yeah, well so do I,' I replied. 'Look, neither of us is entirely happy with this. But you need to do your thing and I need to do mine. And please, stop pretending like everything's okay and I'll be perfectly safe here. You know that's not true.'

Marko looked at me with a resigned expression. As much as he didn't want to see me go, even he could no longer pretend that I would be safe in Zadar.

I wondered about Marko and what was going on in his mind. Why had he chosen this path for himself? I wanted to tell him, so dearly, that all he had to do was abandon everything and stay with me—and I would do the same. Yet I couldn't bring myself to tell him; I felt he needed to realise it himself.

Regardless of everything that had happened, I knew I didn't want to leave Marko. This time it felt different to when I had moved to Zagreb; and we both knew it. I could hardly bring myself to look at his face. His blue eyes were so exhausted and full of worry. Their stares felt heavy on my back as I packed the few remaining essentials I would be taking with me. For a brief moment, I allowed myself to imagine a life where I stayed in Zadar; Marko and I together, like we'd always been.

'Mara,' Marko said in a barely audible whisper. I finally looked into his eyes and saw the desperation in them.

'Marko …' I said, struggling to find the words. 'Please don't make this any harder than it already is.'

'You don't understand …' Marko said.

'No. I suppose I don't.'

I moved towards him and took him into my arms, where we held each other for a while. Despite the reassurances we gave one another, neither Marko nor I truly knew how long it would be before we were together once more. But we had to believe that things would improve soon. Neither of us wanted to face the thought of having to endure a permanent separation.

I needed to leave for the bus station in a few minutes. Mama and Alisa were preparing sandwiches in the kitchen for the bus trip in a pained silence. They were also having a hard time accepting that I was about to leave, even if they were far more reasonable about it all than Marko had been. I was about to zip up my suitcase when I paused.

'Do you remember when you gave me this book?' I asked him, holding up my well-read copy of *The Master and Margarita*.

Marko looked momentarily confused, as though I was transporting him back into another era. 'Yes,' he finally said, with a little smile. 'That was the night we first kissed. As if I could forget.'

'I still have all the books you've gifted me,' I told him. 'All this time … and I never gave you anything.' My bottom lip trembled.

What would Marko have to remember me by? I became distressed and hot tears cut a burning path down my cheeks.

'Mara,' Marko came closer and hugged me, and I could feel his tears dripping onto my hair. He was holding his breath as if he needed to tell me something, but there was only silence.

My boy with smiling eyes, whose face was kind.

As we let go, I had a thought and stepped towards my bookcase. I grabbed the first book my hand moved to; *Nine Stories*, by J. D. Salinger.

'Here,' I said to Marko. 'This one is from me to you.' I'd never even read it myself, but it didn't matter. It was something.

Marko took the book, genuinely grateful.

'Is this your way of getting me into books?' he joked.

'Books are actually amazing, you know.' I said as though I had discovered this secret and finally shared it with him.

'You're probably right.' he said. 'And really, all this time, I've actually just been kind of jealous of books.'

'What?' I laughed. 'Why?'

'Because you were always so in love with them! I figured they must be pretty entertaining then, so … I just had to find ways to be entertaining too.' Marko revealed.

I laughed out loud and Marko chuckled a bit, glad he could still awaken such a response in me. But as we made our way down to the courtyard to say goodbye, I felt sorry for him in a way I never had before. His little insecurities revealed themselves from time to time, only for me to laugh them away.

Down in the gravel courtyard—the place where we had first met as little kids—we kissed each other goodbye.

The bus was to leave late in the evening, make a few stops, and arrive in Sarajevo by early morning. I stared at my mother with a blank, emotionless expression; one of defeat. She stood by my side with my sister nestled in between us. I had to hand it to Mama—she was a master at maintaining a positive guise in the presence of Alisa.

I wished I had the strength to do the same.

'When is Mara coming back?' my sister asked no one in particular.

'Soon, my love,' my mother replied. 'We'll all be together again soon.'

I wanted to believe what my mother was saying, so I did. I would never rid myself of that childish belief that a mother's words were the absolute truth; that whatever she said must be right. I also flashed a smile at my sister, which seemed to satisfy her.

'If things deteriorate here,' my mother said to me in a hushed voice, 'then we'll come and join you at Branislav and Selma's home. Okay? Do not worry, this is all temporary.'

Having chosen to pack lightly, I had one suitcase for all my belongings. Mostly, it was books. Marko's books. The rest of my stuff I left in my bedroom in Zadar. I would come back to it, of course.

I had loaded my single piece of luggage onto the bus and taken the compulsory survival kit of food from my mother. Hot pastries, sandwiches, sweets, juices and fruit all weighed down the plastic bag Mama had handed to me. I felt a pang of unbearable appreciation well up inside my chest, as though I was suddenly overcome with the love my mother had showered me with all my life.

I hugged my mother hard, not wanting to let go. She held me tightly, and I was surprised at the strength in her arms. I released her, only to reach down and hold my sister. I realised then just how little I had to reach; she had grown so much. She was soon to start high school. I thought back to my days at school and how happy I was back then. I wondered whether it could be the same for Alisa.

I took my place on the bus in a window seat. There were very few travellers—mostly elderly people returning to their villages after having visited children or grandchildren in the city. I sat a few seats behind the driver, close to the front of the bus. My mother always told me to do that so that I could keep an eye on the driver, to make sure he wasn't falling asleep. I didn't think this would be the case, for the man was manically puffing away on cigarette after cigarette, whilst taking large chugs of black coffee from a thermos beside him.

'*Ajmo, ajmo!*' The driver called. 'Let's go, I don't have all night!'

The last of the passengers took their seats and made themselves comfortable. The driver started up the bus, put out his cigarette—which had been smoked until only ashes remained—and reversed out of the platform. I waved at my mother and sister who stood outside in the pleasantly warm night. Summer was reluctant to leave, putting off autumn's arrival as much as it could.

I watched until Mama and Alisa disappeared from view, then I focused my attention on the streets that flew by. Zadar began to fall behind us until it, too, was gone from view. We entered the windy roads that were to take us inland, through Lika, and towards the border.

I mostly thought of inconsequential things on the trip; thinking of Marko or my family was too hard. I hoped to hell that my mother's optimism was accurate. I didn't want to worry about the whereabouts and safety of the men and the women in my life who had been left behind. Perhaps it was all exaggerated, this hatred and this paranoia.

Eventually we made it to Lika, and I smiled to myself knowing that close-by, Dida and Baka were safe in their homes. I let my mind wander to happier childhood memories.

'Look at this place,' I heard the driver say to the middle-aged man sitting behind him. 'Just thinking of the filth that lives here makes me sick.' The passenger behind him grunted in agreement.

'Well, they won't be around for much longer,' he responded.

'If I had it my way,' the driver continued, 'I would slit the throat of every last one of them while they slept. Right here, right now.'

The two men laughed in agreement, as I sat frozen in my seat. I couldn't sleep for the rest of the drive, wondering about what was awaiting me in Sarajevo, and whether I could truly escape from this at all.

I made it into Sarajevo during summer's last few breaths. I was ready to exhale after what had felt like months of holding my breath in; but I had barely inhaled the scent of Bosnia's linden trees before the air went stale and got stuck in my throat again.

Almost immediately after my arrival to Sarajevo, Zadar was closed off; restricted. All of Dalmatia had essentially been blocked off from the rest of Croatia.

Mama delivered the news to me during a brief phone conversation. I knew I couldn't go there anyway but being trapped on the outside of Zadar—while everyone I loved was on the inside—felt like another layer of pain poured over me.

Mama said she had not heard from Tata yet, but that could be interpreted as a good sign. None of this was good though. I didn't have the strength to go searching for any victories, however small.

No one was bold enough to say it, but both Mama and I knew very well that we were not going to see each other any time soon. Hopes of returning home, or of being joined by my mother and sister, were now gone. We were in limbo.

My uncle Branislav exchanged a few words with Mama after she had spoken to me. I wondered whether she was saving the truth for his ears only and feeding me a diluted version of events.

But we did not dwell on it.

Uncle Branislav did his best to keep me occupied, knowing all too well that busy hands and busy minds left little room for thinking of much else.

Quite cleverly, my uncle and aunt entrusted me with taking care of Lejla and I did all I could for the little girl. As painful as it was to be reminded of my own little sister, who felt so far away now, I relished my time with my cousin and I knew it helped me get through each day. Lejla was a powerful distraction.

But during the day, while Lejla was at kindergarten, my favourite place to go to was Baščaršija.

Baščaršija was where I could get the best coffee whilst feasting my eyes on the wonders and objects that I passed by; copper coffee grinders, cups and serving ware, precariously stacked up high in shop-fronts; flocks and flocks of pigeons circulating the main square; prayer mats scattered alongside building entryways and mosques. I absorbed it all.

'Have you always lived in Sarajevo?' I asked my aunt Selma while we strolled up to the main square.

'No, I was born and raised in Mostar actually.' she replied.

'Mostar?' I exclaimed. 'Just like my father. He used to take me there when I was really young, before Alisa was born.' I smiled at the memory.

'It's beautiful, isn't it?' Selma said. 'I only left Mostar to go to university in Sarajevo, and then of course that's where I met Branislav. He was also from out of town so we got to know each other by getting to know Sarajevo. He would come and visit me on campus during his breaks from work, and it was lovely. When I graduated, neither of us wanted to leave. We had fallen in love—with each other, and the city!' Selma laughed.

And I could see what she meant. The city had a way of capturing one's heart.

'Should we keep walking to Žuta Tabija?' Selma asked. I nodded and we ventured further uphill to the yellow bastion. From there, we had a wonderful view of the Sarajevo skyline.

'Do you think you know your way around well enough yet?' Selma asked me, joking slightly.

'Um, maybe not quite!' I replied. The city felt enormous. 'But I'll figure it out.' And I knew I would. I had only scratched the surface and there was so much more I wanted to see.

We had come quite far so we eventually made our way back, catching a bus home to the precinct of Grbavica.

My aunt and uncle had cleared out a bedroom just for me, moving my cousin Lejla into their own. I felt guilty, but they had insisted. It was just one of many things they did to settle me in. I couldn't help but notice, every so often, the look of pity my uncle Branislav would give me, or the way Selma fussed over me just that little bit too much. To them, I was a sad case—someone who was without her parents and sibling. To me, it felt like I was some sort of guest of honour in their beautiful city.

Aunt Selma worked in accounting for some government body. It involved quite high-level thinking but was performed around the half-hour coffee breaks and gossip sessions that were a given in every Yugoslav office environment.

My uncle, on the other hand, was a shopkeeper. He had his own business, so he worked hard. I was more than willing to help. I had approached my uncle about joining him at work, for it looked as though I would be hanging around for the unforeseeable future. I felt like a leech, taking everything but contributing nothing.

My first day on the job, I woke early. I made coffee for my uncle and myself, then heated up last night's *burek* for breakfast. We left together, walking the short distance to Branislav's store. It was a *papirnica*, a stationery store mostly filled with school supplies for young students, along with bits and pieces for the office. I had been in there before, just briefly when visiting my uncle or delivering lunch to him. I was not prepared, however, for the uneasy feeling I had once Uncle Branislav opened the shop. *The books, the pens, the atlases, the bags and writing paper.* I was reminded of not so long ago, when I was a student, readying myself for university. Would I ever have that experience again? Would I ever finish what I started?

I sighed and walked around to the counter. Uncle Branislav was going to show me how to operate the register, which would give him more time for the business side of things. Previously he had enlisted the help from their neighbour—a middle-aged widow with two sons. She was a shy but helpful woman, who appreciated the quietness of the store and was always pleasant to customers. Branislav told me she left a month ago, though, and took her sons with her. The woman had an uncle in Germany, which was where they went to. When Branislav asked her why she was leaving after all this time, she said that she had already lost a husband and she was not prepared to lose her sons. He thought her actions drastic.

Business had been good lately, as school had just recently started. There were still plenty of customers—children who realised they were missing a geometry set, paintbrushes or perhaps a diary. A parent—usually the mother—would rush them into the store, commenting on their child's lack of organisation. 'How typical of him. School has started and now he tells me he needs new books. He couldn't have done this weeks ago, could he? And I was trying to save this month's wages, but there goes that idea ...'

My uncle and I would engage in polite conversation, and I would always smile at the children, almost envious of them. We often had high schoolers come in, too, even university students. Sometimes it felt like the entire city was being schooled, apart from me.

Nonetheless, I had regained a sense of purpose. I took pride in my work. I read to Lejla each night and tried to teach her letters and words. We took frequent trips to museums and galleries, and beyond the city to the striking mountain ranges that enveloped us. Winter blessed us with snow that I so rarely got to see back at home, and Sarajevo enchanted me in a way that no other city had done, or ever would. I felt lucky, and I still do, to have lived in this city and to have seen it while it was all in one piece. Before the war came and decimated so much of it.

Chapter 17

In March of 1992 Bosnia declared independence.

I studied my uncle's face as he scanned the headline of the newspaper. He bore such a peculiar expression. A combination of fear, shock and general amazement. And then, a look of acceptance. An expression that admitted defeat to something that had been known all along.

I was fiddling with the tools around his garage while he tended to an old *Zastava* that belonged to a neighbour. In between work, my uncle used his mechanical skills to fix minor car problems for neighbours and friends, which they gave him a bit of cash for. He was inspecting the greasy motor of the vehicle when aunt Selma came in looking restless. She was standing by the garage door, biting on one of her nails, not saying a word. I was holding the tip of a screwdriver onto the workbench, slowly twirling it between my fingers.

'I'm going to get Lejla from kindergarten,' said Selma. She turned to go, shaking her head, clearly carrying out an internal monologue of confusion.

'Ah, comrade Tito,' my uncle sighed. 'If you were only here to see this ...' He stood up and moved towards the *Zastava*, ready to begin fixing the motor that would no doubt stop working again in another six months.

Mama called that evening. She couldn't talk for long, since phone calls were expensive and money seemed to be quickly diminishing for everyone, including my family. Mama had her hours reduced at work, significantly so. When she asked her employers why they had to reduce her working time, especially considering the difficult living conditions everyone was experiencing, they simply replied with 'times are tough for businesses, too'. But she was suspicious. Mama couldn't help but notice that the only employees who were having their hours reduced were those of Serbian background.

'Am I being paranoid, Mara? Is it wrong to think this way?' My mother asked me as though she were the child, seeking reassurance from an adult.

'I don't know, Mama,' I said. 'But nothing surprises me anymore.' I found it all too hard to believe. Despite what was happening, we still had friends in Zadar. My mother had been working in the same place for as long as I could remember, and everyone loved her. She was good at her job. It didn't make sense that people could turn on her, not after so long, not because of something so superficial. But maybe to them, it was far from superficial; maybe it was of dire importance.

'Your Baka Roza believes it is all carefully planned out,' my mother said. 'She thinks it is all part of some greater strategy to "purify" Croatia. But you know her; she is still under the effects of the last World War ...' Mama trailed off, but she left me thinking. I didn't want to think the worst of people by succumbing to judgements and presumptions, but I couldn't afford to continue being so hopeful. I had to consider that my Baka Roza might be right. People were capable of terrible things, as history had shown, and who's to know what evil could present itself in the true characters of individuals?

I finished my conversation with my mother, glad to hear that there was at least no bad news where my father was concerned. Mama and Alisa were lonely, evidently. And although Mama didn't want to admit it directly, they were becoming somewhat ostracised. My sadness quickly gave way to my anger. Where were all those friends of ours? Our neighbours, our colleagues, our comrades? When did my family suddenly become so alone?

That night I could not get to sleep. I started off by thinking of Marko, as I usually do, wondering where he might be and when I would hear from him. But on this evening, more than anyone, I thought of my father. Memory after memory appeared to me before slowly evaporating, and I found myself straining to remember things that I thought I had forgotten long ago. Everything seemed too important to lose now, even the memories.

When I was younger, before I had even started school, I remember asking my father, 'Tata, do you see everything in the colour blue?' I was so amazed by his eyes and the sharpness of their colour that I was convinced his whole world must be painted blue.

'Mara, do you see everything in brown, from those big, dark eyes of yours?' he replied. I considered his question and knew straight away that my father, just like me, saw the world in all its colours and shades. He laughed when he saw the realisation in my face, and when he smiled his eyes glinted and shone all the more.

I understood his logic, but somehow, deep down, I still thought there must be times when the world he sees around him became a reflection of his own two blue eyes; light and pure and beautiful.

I knew he was my father and he was not the same person to everyone, but I struggled to understand how anyone could look into his face and want to hurt him. Tata had no hatred inside of him, and I wished so much that it would be enough for others to see that. I fell asleep hoping this, but dreamt instead of terrible things throughout the entire, restless night.

I awoke in the morning to thoughts of Marko. I must have been dreaming of him in the early hours, because his face was still imprinted in my mind. But it wasn't the adult Marko. It was Marko as a little boy, and we were running into the water together at

Petrčane beach. He was ahead of me and I was calling him, but he wouldn't turn around. He dived into the water and disappeared. I called out again, but nothing. I went to dive in after him, but that was when I woke up.

My heart was racing and I took a moment to come to my senses. I got up out of bed and began my daily routine, wishing away thoughts of Marko that hurt too much to bear.

But, on that day it was though I had conjured him from my dreams, because when the mail arrived in the afternoon, so did a letter. It was from Marko.

The next day, there was another one.

And then the letters wouldn't stop coming.

He wrote consistently, yet I replied sporadically at best, barely able to keep up with the arrival of each new letter. It didn't deter him. For all the writing Marko had avoided during school, he was very well making up for it now.

Mostly, he spoke of his memories of the two of us, which was the hardest thing to read about. But of course, he finished every letter with talk of 'our' nation's struggle—full of optimism and stories of the front lines. It made me think that all we shared in these letters were memories—for our present was no longer the two of us.

He spoke of the skirmishes that took place on Zadar's outskirts, and of heading further inland. He said he had helped 'liberate' our city. Liberate from whom, I wondered. From families like mine? From people like myself?

I was stunned, but also curious. And I couldn't help it. I missed him, and I wanted to hear from him. So, when I could, I wrote back.

I addressed all the letters to the apartment where Marko had grown up, not knowing if the letters would ever arrive and whether they would be passed on to him. He managed to get all his letters to me somehow, even if they sometimes arrived very late or not in order of when they were written. I kept them all, gently folded in my copy of *The Little Prince*. The illustration of the little prince on the cover even kind of reminded me of a young Marko. How fitting. A little boy, so lonely and seemingly lost in this world.

Originally, I feared that I would have nothing to tell Marko. But the war was starting to produce more and more material to write about. I asked Marko whether he had heard of the killings up north, in places like Sijekovac and surrounding regions, and whether it was true that they were targeting Serbs. I asked whether he was anywhere near the conflict. I then asked him about Bijeljina, and what was being done to the Bosniaks, and I wondered how many people were caught in the middle of this nationalist euphoria erupting on all sides. It was as if I was expecting an explanation to arrive, from Marko of all people, as a way of making sense of the senselessness.

But these questions never warranted a response, and I had no way of knowing why.

I had many more questions to ask but I also feared the answers. And when I saw that my efforts were getting me nowhere, eventually I stopped asking.

Then one day, there were no more letters from Marko. As suddenly as they had appeared, they had ceased; no letters on that day, nor any day thereafter. A creeping dread consumed me and settled deep within my bones.

As though it had followed me from my home, fear and angst made its way through Sarajevo and manifested in all the worst ways. It was like a volcano had been bubbling away, spitting out hot ashes here and there, spilling lava on pockets of our land and sometimes burning victims in moments of cruelty. And then the real eruption started; in the heart of our nation, where the volcano found its fury.

Sarajevo was burning.

The mountains encircling the city were like a haze, flickering in the smoke that consumed the air. It had grown so quickly, from isolated attacks and conflicts, to entire towns and cities coming under siege.

Quite quickly my fears for my family back home had diminished into fears for my own self. I was meant to be the one who was safest, but instead I had positioned myself as a sitting duck in the conflict between our brothers and sisters.

The shelling of Sarajevo lasted for days. Bullet after bullet was being fired. I felt like my head was constantly being hammered; that all too familiar chest pain arose within me. I strained to breathe, even to think. Sweat poured down me like I was standing under a cold shower; it was the sweat of fear, of uncertainty. Of knowing only one thing, and that was that people were dying.

A loud rumbling in the distance startled me into holding my breath, and I begged for some silence, or an end to it all. My uncle and cousin were sitting opposite to me, exchanging fearful and tentative looks. Lejla was on my uncle's lap, and his arms were around her like a protective shield. That was the best he could do. He must have felt so helpless as her father. I imagined my father felt something similar, if he was able to feel anything anymore. I wished I was in Tata's arms right now, and the thought made me start sobbing.

Another rumble, this time louder. I closed my eyes.

I didn't try to contain my trembling hands. Then, for the first time in my life, I prayed. I prayed to God, to Allah, to Buddha. I prayed to Zeus. Despite my efforts, no God answered. Maybe the higher powers didn't listen to atheists.

What was I even thinking? Prayer?! Perhaps I was losing my mind. I could think now of only one thing as I sat on the sinking two-seater sofa, head in my hands in a pool of cold sweat. Words came to my head. Music came to my head.

> *'Yugoslavia, on your feet …*
> *Sing so they can hear you …'*

A loud explosion reverberated around the room. I looked up quickly at my uncle, who had his hands covering his daughter's ears.

> *'Who doesn't listen to the song …*
> *Will listen to the storm …'*

I hummed another tune to myself, one I vaguely remembered. I remembered it from some time ago, when I lived in a nice apartment. It had a big courtyard with kids always playing in it. I think there was a café on the corner, but I wasn't sure anymore. So, I continued to hum the tune because I was sure it once existed. Something must have.

'My Balkans, be strong for me, and stay well …'

The gunfire was subsiding. The apartment shook for the last time. The window rattled. I remained focused on the wall opposite of where I sat. I could hear my uncle attempting to calm my cousin, to tell her that it was over now.

The phone rang. My uncle jumped up to go and answer it, and I got up and grabbed Lejla in my arms. Christ, what was a child her age meant to make of all this? In the other room, I heard my uncle crying, but they were tears of relief. Aunt Selma was safe, still at her mother's place. Everyone was ok. She was on her way home and Branislav told her to be careful on her way back. To beware of snipers. He came back into the room and grabbed both Lejla and I, holding us tight and not letting go for a long time.

The shots rang louder than the church bells at noon. It was late at night and I was lying in bed. I knew the shots were not close by, but knowing the bullets were hitting targets far from where I lay brought no comfort. There had been times when the bullets had come close enough to scatter the walls of the building with an uneven arrangement of holes, like a poor-quality dot-painting had been chiselled into them. I had ventured out the next day, after the first time I felt the bullets hit our building. I had scaled my fingers over the small holes which now scarred the brightly coloured walls, studying the small cracks that spread outwards from where the bullets had hit in a spider web-like pattern.

Nonetheless, I, like everyone else in the city, had adapted to the sights and sounds. Eventually the sleepless nights became less frequent and the atmosphere somewhat bearable; bearable enough to be able to fall asleep. Somehow, just knowing that everyone was at home and in bed provided some relief.

On this night, though, I was feeling that same fear I had felt at the start of all the chaos.

I heard the key turn in the door. Then my uncle's familiar footsteps entered the hallway and I breathed a long sigh of relief. I turned over in my bed and looked out the window, into the darkness. Every so often a flash of orange light could be seen in the distance.

'Mara?' my uncle whispered. He had opened the door to my room ever so slightly, allowing a faint glow to enter. I pretended to be asleep. I could feel him standing by the door, still watching over me. It made me feel safe. A minute or so later he closed the door and left. I could hear him getting into bed, no doubt next to his equally as sleepless and tired wife.

Finally, the exhaustion consumed me and I drifted into a deep sleep. The bullets raged on in the distance. They were close, but they could be closer. I wanted to get out of here. I *had* to get out of here.

I fell asleep that night with the stack of Marko's letters under my pillow.

Sometimes you would walk into a scene without even realising. You'd walk right in, before any emergency services even arrived and before you could even see any signs of carnage. You would hear some yelling and shouting, but that was not uncommon so you wouldn't think much of it. The first real giveaway is the stony silence.

It was just a street like any other; a supermarket, a few *trafika* stands and not much else. As soon as I thought that something had happened, that things couldn't possibly be this quiet and this noisy at the same time, I should have just closed my eyes and turned around. Yet I rounded the corner and saw a body on the ground; there were more bodies but I didn't get that far. I inhaled a sudden, cold breath and let my eyes linger longer than I should have.

Then I stepped back behind the corner and pressed my back up the wall with my eyes firmly closed.

Oh God, oh God, oh God.

Slowly but inevitably, the sounds of others started pouring in. An ambulance siren. Some helpful civilians emerging and issuing directions. And the moaning. Some hadn't died yet. Maybe they would be saved.

I think it was a man I had seen. I wondered how old he was. I wondered what he had been doing. I bet he didn't think it would be his last day alive.

Tears stung my cheeks and my ears felt burning hot. The scene started getting noisier and people were rushing past me. I swallowed the creeping nausea back into my stomach and, ever so slowly, dragged my legs in the opposite direction.

I felt a strange sense of guilt for not even checking on the man. But in my mind, I knew it would have been pointless. *Don't be silly.* I said to myself. *You saw straight away that his face was unrecognisable.*

Somehow, I found my way home.

'Where have you been?' my uncle asked me. 'You've been gone for ages. I got worried.'

He sounded angry. I looked up at him and realised by the dimness of the light that it was already quite late. I couldn't account for the last few hours. Uncle Branislav must have sensed it, since he came and ushered me towards the sofa to sit down. Minutes later he brought me a sweet, hot rosehip tea and sat down next to me, with an arm around my shoulder.

'I saw a body.' I blurted out.

'Yes, I thought you might have,' my uncle said, looking downwards. We didn't speak for a long time.

The taste of bile filled my mouth. I didn't even care. I drained the tea and imagined it washing everything away.

'Mara.' Branislav said abruptly, as though he had just had a revelation. 'We will get you out of here.'

We finally made eye contact. He looked so sincere.

'Out of Sarajevo?'

My uncle nodded. I hadn't thought of leaving, up until this moment. Well, up until a few hours ago, when I realised I had seen too much.

'You know, Mara, I was always drawn more to mountains and green fields than I ever was to the sea. I guess that's why when the time came to leave Lika, I chose to come to Sarajevo.' Branislav said. He looked at me and raised his eyebrows. I figured this was his way of telling me that he couldn't leave.

I get it. I know what it's like to love a place as though it were a person.

But Sarajevo had become something wholly different to what it once was.

'And look what we've done to it.' Branislav said more to himself than to me, choking on the last word.

It was a particular kind of hurt, seeing your city burn.

And though my uncle was prepared to go down in flames with it, he intended nothing of the sort to happen to me.

I just had to survive one more evening here before I could get out of Sarajevo for good. I had a window of opportunity—a ceasefire—to get out of the city. Ceasefires had been broken before, but I had to take this next chance. Uncle Branislav knew someone he believed could get me out of here safely, and only because I was a Serb. This didn't seem fair to me, but nothing was fair. Branislav wanted me to leave, even when he knew his family stood no chance.

When my last day arrived, I didn't even say goodbye properly, because I was done with goodbyes. Just a 'see you next time'. It felt less permanent this way. 'See you', to my generous aunt and uncle. 'See you' to little Lejla with the dimple on her right cheek.

Please don't die, I thought to myself, but dared not say aloud.

I left with my uncle, heading further east into the city where my ride was waiting. We walked the longer but safer route, and even then, the signs of conflict were impossible to ignore. I looked around at this city with its light extinguished and its people sunken and fearful. It felt like someone had taken the Mona Lisa and scribbled all over it with a permanent marker. Defaced it with no mercy.

As we approached the bus on this unusually cool evening, I hitched up my backpack a bit higher and wrapped my jacket closer. Like a snail with only its fragile little shell to hide in, I sank into myself and tried not to make eye contact with the sniper standing nearby.

Branislav made quick conversation with the man and then nodded towards me. They exchanged something between their hands, and that was that. The sniper gestured with his head towards the bus.

We were so tense and agitated at the same time. My uncle gave me the tightest, shortest hug he could, knowing we had no time to waste and that anything could happen in an instant. It was a sharp hug but full of care. Like a vaccination. I clung to the feeling of this hug as though it were the only protection I had for the journey ahead.

I took my seat and looked out the window for my uncle, but he was already gone. I rested my head on my backpack which was nestled in my lap. I wished for my parents, and my parents' parents.

The bus taking us across the border and into Serbia was not in the best shape, nor were the people travelling on it. Everyone looked haggard and frightened, even though we had already been given clearance and a safe passage to get out.

I thought I would find peace in Sarajevo, and yet the war had come closest to me there. I kept thinking of my uncle, aunt and cousin, and whether I would see them again. I felt as though the conflict was following me. Every time I left one place for another, war arrived soon after. Surely, I was cursed.

Chapter 18

I took another puff, pretending to enjoy every moment of it. Even with the sanctions, cigarettes were always possible to come by. I had taken up the habit for God knows what reason. Nothing I did anymore had any real motive behind it. I wasn't the only one of my cohort to be seen on a regular basis lazing around Belgrade University campus smoking. It was like a hobby of all of ours.

The discussions that occurred were often as trivial as our actions, with very few students meeting on the campus grounds to discuss politics or philosophy. The closest we got to any political discussion was the rage expressed towards the European Football Championships that had taken place over the summer, where the Yugoslav team had been banned from playing only ten days prior to the tournament. While most of the country usually followed football religiously, this time around there wasn't as much interest in *Euro 1992*, what would have otherwise been a huge event in Europe.

I was annoyed, but not surprised. I was not naïve to what the rest of Europe thought of Yugoslavia. We weren't even allowed to play football with the big kids, because we were too immature carrying out wars and fighting. Still, I failed to see how useful it was to take away one of the few things Yugoslavia had left to celebrate. I couldn't help but imagine that if things were different, I would have spent the summer at home in my apartment with Marko, our eyes glued to the television as we watched our team make its way to the finals. For some reason, I was certain that Yugoslavia would have won.

But obviously no one could ever know that. Not now.

There were few things that still took me by surprise, as I had grown to expect the unexpected. But every so often things would take a radical change and I'd find myself in a situation I hadn't seen coming. Ever since I had left Zadar, events already put into motion had taken away any control I had over my life. I couldn't really imagine how different things might have been had I stayed in Zadar, or Zagreb, or even Sarajevo.

What was most surprising, though, was not that I had found myself here, smoking and sometimes drinking while the sun was still up, but that I was here at all. Even knowing I'd be returning to Belgrade, I didn't think I would find a way to return to my education. Even when the opportunity presented itself, I felt reluctant to take it.

'You should go back to school,' Aunt Dragana had told me. 'You need some structure in your life.' I had been in Belgrade for all of two weeks and already she was throwing me a pity party.

I had been lucky this time around, for it looked as though at least the conflict was not going to reach us here. On the other hand, Belgrade was no easy place to live in. Times were tough, necessities were scarce, and unpredictability overshadowed every aspect of life.

'Even if I wanted to go back to studying, which I don't, with what money would I support myself?' I was not in the mood for being convinced into any sort of meaningful activity.

'Don't be silly,' Aunt Dragana replied. 'Like anyone is concerned about money these days. Enrol, get started, and everything else will sort itself out. And of course, there are always connections.'

I looked at my aunt, ready for an argument, but then thought otherwise. Her son and daughter were no longer at home—they were adults too after all. Here, my aunt was alone, with only my tormented self for company.

'Whatever you want, *tetka*,' I said, finally caving in.

Aunt Dragana was being serious when she had mentioned her connection. I soon found myself meeting the man who would provide me with an obstacle-free passage back into higher education.

'And I know exactly who you are. You look a little like your grandmother, believe it or not.' I had walked into the living room having woken up only moments ago. I looked at the clock, which said it was already ten past eleven. 'You're going to have to start waking up earlier than this if you want to make it to your classes on time.'

I looked at the man who had spoken to me, not quite sure of what he was talking about. He and Aunt Dragana were sitting at the dining table, drinking Turkish coffees and eating *ratluk*. I went over to join them.

'Mara, this is Mr Todorović,' my aunt told me.

'But you can call me Milan,' the man said.

'Nice to meet you,' I said to him, feeling slightly awkward.

'Milan,' my aunt went on, 'is an old friend of ours who just happens to work at the university. I thought you might have a few things to discuss with him.'

'An old *friend*?' I enquired. I didn't recall ever hearing any mention of this man, yet here he was, in what appeared to be a casual tea party with my aunt. He was not that much older than her, but far younger than my grandparents, it appeared. I couldn't figure out how he fitted into the picture.

'What, no one's ever told you?' Milan asked. 'Well I suppose it's not surprising, seeing how humble your grandparents are.' My look of confusion must have told him I didn't quite understand what he was alluding to, prompting him to explain.

'I owe my life to your Baka and Dida, the parents of your dear mother and aunt and uncle,' Milan said. 'When they found me, the war had already been going for two years. I was but seven years old, orphaned and close to death. The Ustashe had killed my family, but I had managed to escape. However, it was not long before the cold weather and lack of food left me tired and malnourished, with only an old barn as refuge. Your grandparents found me and took me in. They themselves had nowhere safe to go, and yet they found a place in their hearts for me.'

I listened on, surprised by what I was hearing. I was not prepared for a discussion about the events of World War Two this early in the day.

'We ended up in *Jasenovac* concentration camp, and even then, your Baka Anka kept me safe. She passed me off as her nephew and treated me as her own. We survived that camp; we eventually made it out and began a new life in Lika. When I turned fifteen, I left to go and find work. I felt I had to repay your grandparents for everything, but of course, they didn't accept a cent from me. When I found my way to Belgrade and was blessed with success, I promised them they could always count on me for anything.'

'I remember Milan, just a bit,' Aunt Dragana said. 'But your mum was quite young and probably has no memory of him, and your uncle wasn't even born by the time Milan had left. I suppose it always remained as something between Milan and your grandparents,' more than anything.'

I was truly at a loss for words. I didn't know what else to do but smile. I felt a burst of longing for my grandparents, those quiet heroes who never spoke of their decency and bravery. What else was there that I didn't know about them? Or was it that I had never cared to ask?

'Well, Mileva, I haven't forgotten anything,' Milan interrupted my thoughts. 'And I'm here now to help put you through school. It is the least I could do. I expect no resistance from you, this has already been decided. I will inform you as to when you will commence your studies.' He said this with sincerity, but with strict overtones. I simply nodded and thanked him, not sure of what to think.

Mr Todorović thanked my aunt and left the apartment. It wasn't until later that I thought more about my grandparents and what they had been through. They had survived the Second World War. And now the cruel hand of destiny had brought war back into their lives and homes yet again. I hoped I had inherited at least an iota of their resilience.

I found myself in the lecture halls of Belgrade University, the old classrooms and laboratories providing me with new home away from home. As reluctant as I had initially been, I had to admit that I was incredibly relieved to find myself studying once more. Aunt Dragana had done right by me and I knew I owed her. But I made a point of neglecting to mention the bad habits I had picked up within my new social circle.

What was to be expected? My generation had been left stranded and disillusioned. The students still studied, just like the workers still worked and the politicians still 'governed'. We had no other way to pass our time than to bask in the decadence of life's simple and unhealthy pleasures. Cigarette after cigarette was consumed. One beer after another. Sometimes we went to class but sometimes we simply didn't bother turning up. From the outside, we probably appeared apathetic. But there were still those on campus who protested, who demanded action and who wanted to be heard.

I didn't bother.

There was nowhere for people to go. There were no holidays to plan for, no big careers to dream of. And thanks to inflation, it had become nearly impossible to buy just about anything. One day when I was at the corner market, I found myself unable to afford a banana to eat. It felt so unjust. *A banana!* I wasn't even after a *bunch* of bananas. Just one would have been enough.

Our currency was useless and our supplies were little. I kept up my schedule of studying because it was all I had. It gave me a purpose, but I wondered every day, what was I studying for? I saw no end to any of it. I saw no career at the end of my academic accomplishments. The only people profiting during times like these were criminals and politicians. And it would stay that way for a very long time to come.

And, predictably so, there were really only two people I needed back in my life; Tata and Marko. And I couldn't be sure of where either of them was.

I came home one Thursday, after being at university, to find my aunt sitting in the living room with Nenad. My cousin immediately came over and gave me a hug. Nenad's eyes looked older, and his five o'clock shadow was testament to his growth into adulthood. He wasn't so much my partying, rebellious cousin anymore, as he was a man with the weight of the world on his shoulders. Still so very young though. Far too much weight for such young shoulders. I went down and sat next to my aunt on the sofa. She looked worried.

Nenad had set the table for dinner and had started pouring hot soup into three bowls.

'Your mother called,' my aunt said. I looked at her, waiting for details. 'Some not so good news from Zadar ... nothing terrible,' she said after seeing my face freeze. 'But not very good.' Nenad was looking at the floor, frowning.

'Your mother has lost her job,' Aunt Dragana said. 'They are receiving no money from your father's work, so now they have nothing.' I considered this. My mother, unemployed and living alone with my sister. 'Before you start to panic, do not fear. We have made arrangements,' she explained.

I wondered what sort of arrangements could possibly help repair this situation. So much was being lost and so fast.

'Your mother has gone to Lika. She has helped Baka and Dida pack up their things so that they may move to Zadar. They will be living in your apartment from now on. This is better anyway, as we don't trust what is going on outside of the cities ...' I failed to see how this was a helpful arrangement and asked Aunt Dragana to continue to the point.

'Sanja and Alisa will then move here, to Belgrade. They will have to go via Slovenia and bypass Croatia and will come here from the north, from Hungary.'

'They're coming here? To live with us?' I had momentarily forgotten my mother's strife and thought instead of being reunited with her and my sister.

'Yes, they will live here with us. It will be cosy for a little while, but we are family, so we'll stay together for as long as we need to.' It made sense. I wondered why we hadn't thought of this earlier. We could have all been living in Belgrade.

As though she knew what I was thinking my aunt said, 'Your mum didn't want to leave Zadar. But this was the last straw. I think she was holding onto her home out of stubbornness and spite, but conditions have worsened. And getting to Serbia won't be easy. But we do still have *some* friends at least.'

I knew then how it would have felt for my mother: *defeat*. My father was gone, I had left, and now finally her and Alisa. Even my grandparents had to leave their home in Lika. I wondered what would become of Baka and Dida's home in Lika. It would probably get looted, if not destroyed by nationalists. They had done just that to our home in the *selo*, one day when Dmitar was not there. They knew exactly who was living there, but I guess that was the point.

I also thought about my Baka Roza. Who did she have left? Soon we were all to be gone from Zadar, and her only son was still at war.

I spoke to my mother one more time, the night before she and Alisa were due to leave Zadar. Her voice was emotionless and exhausted.

'I have packed some of your belongings as well, I thought you might want them,' Mama said to me.

'You didn't need to do that, Mama. I have everything I need. Don't burden yourselves with useless stuff when you need to pack as much as of your own things as you can,' I told her.

'Don't worry, it's just some things you might like to have. So you don't forget,' she replied, her voice quivering. I thanked her for doing so, but I wasn't sure if I wanted any old memories coming back to me.

But then …

'Also, I have to tell you something. I ran into Marko's mother the other day,' she said. I felt myself holding my breath for a moment before remembering to exhale. Mama sensed I was listening and continued.

'She looks like a broken woman, Mara. We couldn't talk for long because she feared that someone might see her with me and think the wrong thing. They all know her boy is fighting for the nation and all that, and here she is speaking to a Serb. It was brave of her, really, to even approach me. But she said she had to. She wanted to know how we are and most of all, how you are.'

I was breathing quickly now, a surge of emotions flooding my mind. I wanted to cry so much, and to hug the woman who loved me so dearly and whose son I loved.

'I told her that you were all right and that you were living in Belgrade now. I gave her Dragana's address. She insisted. She wanted to be able to get in contact, just in case. I guess like all of us, she's prepared for the worst,' Mama said.

I could hardly bring myself to say it, but I had to ask. 'Does she hear at all from Marko?'

'Sometimes, but very rarely,' Mama said. 'Only when he gets the chance, and he doesn't say much. She said he is always asking about you.'

This last statement was like a dagger to the heart. *Dear Marko*. How little I had stopped to think of him. How purposefully I had tried to push him to the depths of my mind. And yet he still missed me.

But of course I missed him, too.

'Okay, Mara, I have to go,' Mama said. 'I will see you soon, *ljubavi*.' I said goodbye and hung up the phone, hopeful that my family would soon be reunited.

The next morning, I rose earlier than I had to. My night had been full of dreams of Marko—but the Marko of my childhood again. We were six years old again and about to start school. Our friendship was still in its early stages of teasing each other and running around together in the courtyard. Then suddenly a car pulls up, Marko gets in and the car drives away. I find I can't move or run. I'm left standing alone in the courtyard and everything has gone dark. That's when I woke up. It was nearly six in the morning, and the sky was starting to lighten up.

I found I had a few *dinars* in my pocket and I thought I would treat myself to a coffee on my way to university. I made sure I had my books with me, especially the paper that was due that day. So far, I had been consistent at playing the good student. I had a few harsh professors but most of them were quite nice. My professor for biology was the loveliest, so I always made an effort in her class. She had been impressed with my work, and I explained to her that I studied quite hard during my first year of university in Zagreb. All of that knowledge must have really stuck, because it was definitely making it easier for me now.

Despite being so prepared for my studies today, I still managed to be late to class. I had gotten so caught up in walking the streets of Belgrade, remembering Marko and myself as courtyard children. I wondered about what he might look like now.

'Zara,' my biology professor said to me once the class had finished. Everyone else was packing up and I was still sitting there. My professor had taken to calling me 'Zara', the Italian name for Zadar. When she found out I was from there she couldn't help but tell me how much she loved that 'most beautiful of towns'.

'I know you're enthusiastic, but class is over. You can go home now,' she said.

I bowed my head and smiled, got up to go and said goodbye as I made my way out of the classroom.

I could now think only of the boy with smiling eyes, whose face was kind.

Time was ticking painfully slowly and the news continued to show the horror. Nenad told me he believed we were being drip fed only a selection of events and updates, and the true atrocities were being hidden from us. It was easy from our vantage point in Belgrade to minimise the war and conflict, or to shift blame away, but I only had to remember my time in Sarajevo to be reminded of how gruesome things were.

So, it was with bated breath that I journeyed to the central bus station on the day I was meant to see my mother and my sister after nearly two years. I had butterflies in my stomach as though I was about to head out on a first date. The weather was sweet, heralding them nicely into the city, but I was cautious of adopting false hope. I wouldn't believe anything until I saw them for myself. This felt too fortunate. Too desired. Too lucky.

It felt odd to be the one not getting *off* the bus this time.

Like out of a movie, a flock of pigeons took off into the air as my mother and sister emerged from the masses, scanning the crowds for my face. I had a moment to myself before they saw me, and I didn't dare move. My mother's curly hair was frizzy, her face a little thinner than I remember. But still so beautiful.

And when she saw me, and smiled, I wanted to believe it was my same Mama as always. That elegant, sassy woman who could do it all.

When my mother grabbed me and hugged me though, there was a desperation in her embrace that I had never felt before. She had conceded to a level of vulnerability that all mothers always carry; that fear of loss. I hugged her back, doing all I could to reassure her that she had never lost me at all.

I watched my mother's face as she unpacked our last few belongings into the hallway cupboard of her sister's apartment. I wondered what had happened to the woman I used to know. Her expression had been replaced by one of defeat, of exhaustion and surrender. To me, my mother used to be the epitome of strength, of independence, of wit and intelligence. How suddenly these traits had been quashed from her. How suddenly she had morphed into a human which simply functioned rather than lived. I helped her pack away the few remaining dregs of our previous life from an old and battered suitcase.

I could see my mother and her sister relying on one another more than ever now. They were unified in their aloneness and found solace in their joint grief.

Mama spent much of her time arranging the few meagre items and possessions she had managed to bring to Belgrade. Apart from practical things like clothing and personal documents, she also brought a few sentimental objects like toys from my childhood, or gifts that Tata had bought her. I was most grateful when I saw that she had remembered the picture Aco had painted for me; the one Nikola had given to me for my birthday. I immediately placed it on my bedside table so I could wake up to it each day.

My sister was noticeably different too. She was far more subdued than I remembered her being. She told me she had no friends left behind in Zadar. A couple of her peers had remained friendly towards her, but nothing beyond politeness.

Not long before the new school year was due to start, I took Alisa along to the local *gimnazija* for her orientation day. She was outwardly nervous.

'Don't worry,' the principal of the school had told us. 'She's not the first refugee we've received from Croatia and she surely won't be the last.'

Chapter 19

It was always about the connections in this country of ours. Yet no matter how many we had, it was insufficient in finding a steady job for Mama. My mother hated dependency. She always had. From a young age she was telling me not to ever be dependent on anyone or anything, especially when it came to finances. 'Don't you ever rely on a man for money, and if you get married, make sure to have your own bank account.' This piece of advice had always stuck with me.

I was happy to have my mother and sister back, of course, but it wasn't the kind of joy I was expecting. It was strange having them here without Tata. The picture felt incomplete. And it was not the sort of family I remembered. Everyone and everything had changed, and I suspected that I, too, had changed.

Uncle Miki came and visited us a few times upon hearing the news that Mama and Alisa had also moved to Belgrade. His visits were a blessing, for he always brought an abundance of supplies from the farm. I don't think even he knew how desperate we were for such basics. It was good to see Miki, and not just because of the food he brought with him. He had changed the least of all. Some people didn't change and managed to see the positive side of life regardless of the harsh reality.

I gave Miki a big hug every time he left to return to his town, but I never told him of how important it was for me to know he would always stay the same.

Relief came in the form of a phone call from Nikola.

'Really, it's about time you came and visited,' he said to me. He was absolutely right. I was relishing in the opportunity to see him and to tell him about everything that had been happening, with my mother and sister and with my thoughts about Marko.

'Ok, I will try and get away for a weekend,' I said to Nikola. 'But it will be hard. We have hardly any money and more mouths to feed now.'

'I understand. Just come whenever you can,' he replied. So I started saving every spare *dinar* I could find. With some help from Aunt Dragana (who took pity on me) I managed to save enough for a return train ticket to Novi Sad.

Mama was happy for me to go, if only because she knew how close Nikola and I had always been. She was grateful I still had a friend. But I could see every day, simply having me around was very important to her. I made sure to stay away for only a few days before returning to Belgrade.

The train ride felt quick, if not bumpy. But all I could think about was Nikola. Had he changed? Did he look the same? I wondered about Ana too, with whom I had had no contact at all for so long. What on earth have their lives been like?

But, when I walked out into Novi Sad's *Železnička Stanica*, it was impossible not to recognise him.

Nikola was the same.

I jumped into his arms and laughed. Nikola hugged me whilst calling out my name in total disbelief. He looked amazing, so healthy and handsome. I had grown used to the downtrodden faces of those around me. People were struggling, naturally. Nikola was not living the high life either, but he didn't need a lot to be satisfied.

I sobbed a little as we hugged and I remembered that day where

Nikola and I cracked eggs together for Orthodox Easter. I so hoped that my wish had come true.

We took a taxi to Nikola's apartment in the suburb of *Liman 2*, which was nestled in between the city centre and the Danube River. Nikola still lived there with his mother, who actually began to cry when she saw me. I found it hard not to do the same. I had not felt so overwhelmed by love in a long time.

Immediately food was served; hot lunch, dessert and coffee afterwards. The conversation didn't stop. Nikola's mother was looking good, considering everything she had been through. She had a job (which was lucky for these times) and she still kept receiving her pay cheque (which was even luckier). Nikola was close to finishing university and was doing some work as an assistant within his faculty. Nikola was as smart as ever, and he had the work ethic of a war horse.

After coffee, Nikola and I headed out for a walk along the *Kej*—the path that follows the Danube around the city.

'I know you've been dying to ask me,' Nikola said. 'So I will confirm that yes, I do have a girlfriend.'

I laughed out loud. 'What are you talking about? It didn't even occur to me to ask …' I said, looking at him innocently.

'Of course, I don't believe you, and now I know you want to know all about her.'

'You're totally right, go on,' I said.

Nikola told me about his girlfriend, whose name was Jovana. They had been dating for over a year already.

'I would have told you earlier, but you know me,' he conceded. 'Not to mention things have been pretty hectic in this here part of the world…'

I didn't mind. He sounded really happy. Jovana seemed like a great person—she had to be if Nikola saw something in her. After mentioning her, though, he suddenly couldn't talk about anything else. As we walked towards the city centre Nikola was still regaling me with stories of his beloved.

He suddenly stopped. 'Sorry, Mara, I didn't realise,' he said.

'Realise what?'

'That I'm talking so much and that all of this probably just reminds you of Marko.'

I hadn't really thought of it that way, but Nikola interpreted my silence as agreement.

'It's okay,' he said. 'I've said enough anyway. You know we don't have to talk about Marko, but we can if you like.'

I wasn't sure where to go from there. It felt like if we were to enter that discussion, it would open up a whole Pandora's Box.

'There isn't a lot to say, Nikola,' was all I could muster. And it was true. What was I going to say? Thoughts of Marko only sent me on an emotional rollercoaster—looping between loving and missing him, to reminding myself of the hurt and disappointment he had caused me.

'You must think I'm an idiot,' I said to my friend.

Nikola looked at me curiously, genuinely confused. 'Why would you think that? In what way are you an idiot?'

'Because of Marko,' I replied. 'Because I should realise that what we had is over and I am still trying to hold on to someone who's really just a memory. I know he changed into a different person. I know that he betrayed me, in a sense. So why is it that I can't stop thinking about him? Why do I still believe that he is not *bad*? That it is impossible for Marko to ever be a *bad* person? That we're still just the same; two children playing in the courtyard?'

My heart was beating fast and I grew frustrated at myself for getting carried away so easily. Then Nikola grabbed my hands in his and looked straight at me, shaking his head slowly.

At once, I knew that I was safe.

'It's because Marko *isn't* a bad person. We all know that. Mara, you are far from idiotic. You are not crazy. You are not wrong,' he said to me. 'What you are is simply a good person who refuses to give up on the good in others. You love Marko and he loves you. But Marko is a young man who is lost, and it is not up to you to guide him back. He doesn't see the conflict between loving you and fighting in this war. To Marko, it is not a fight against anyone in particular. It is a fight against his own lack of purpose, against what he believes are his inadequacies.'

'Was I not enough of a purpose?' I asked feebly.

Nikola looked at me then lowered his gaze.

'Mara,' he said finally. 'People are complicated. Don't be surprised by how those closest to us are often the ones who hurt us most. It makes you doubtful and confused, but it is not personal. People need to find their own path, and many can do so quite easily. But Marko … he was never any good on his own … and it wasn't until he lost you that he began to stray from his path.'

And I realised then that maybe Marko had seen things differently. Maybe he felt that I had abandoned him by leaving for Zagreb. And had I? Up until that point, he and I had always been together. We supported each other for so long. The moment when we were finally separated, things fell apart.

'If you want my advice, Mara,' Nikola said. 'Then just let it go. Don't forget to live your life, because you will only be left with regret.'

Nikola said those words to me with complete compassion in his voice. He wasn't being dismissive but honest. And as always, Nikola was right. There was nothing I could do now about something that happened long ago. I was incapable of changing people's minds, and that included Marko's. I needed to stop being sad and angry. I hoped I could do as Nikola said, and just let it go.

We spent the remainder of the evening in the city centre, where Nikola treated me to a few drinks and introduced me to some friends of his. For one short night, I felt like I was living the life any person my age ought to be living. We talked about things like films and music. Nikola's friends shared anecdotes and funny stories; no talk of war and hunger.

We ended up spending most of the weekend like that, completely carefree. Nikola showed me some of the sights and was a masterful tour guide. I teased him about his accent, which had taken on the typical north Serbian characteristic of slowly dragging out one's words. He was even beginning to adopt the Serbian dialect. It was during my last few hours with Nikola, when I had brought up his new speech patterns once more, that he gave me a sort of serious look.

'Do you hear much from Ana?' Nikola asked me.

'No,' I replied. 'We've never managed to get a phone call together, and apart from a few postcards that she sent to my address in Zadar, there's been nothing.'

'I don't hear from anyone back home,' Nikola said, matter-of-factly. He didn't seem upset by this. His gaze reflected a sort of steely resolve.

'Mara, don't get me wrong,' he said to me, 'but I am trying so hard to forget Zadar.'

I looked at my friend, and I saw his cheerfulness dissipate. 'It's not just because of the sad memories from there, Mara,' he continued. 'It's because of everything that has happened. Our hometown doesn't want us anymore. It will never be home again. This is my home now, and I will act and talk as though it's all I've ever known.'

I nodded gently but didn't say anything. I understood how he felt, but I hadn't reached that stage yet myself.

'I wish I could be like you, Nikola,' I said. 'I wish I could draw a line, cross it, and never go back. Maybe one day that will happen for me.'

'Well, it's probably already happening,' Nikola said. 'I'm not the only one who has picked up a new way of talking. You're a bit too convincing with your Belgrade accent.'

I laughed at him and relaxed a bit more. When Nikola said it, he didn't make it sound so bad. I didn't need to resist, I realised. I admired Nikola and how he had taken control of his own happiness. I needed to do the same.

'Mara,' Nikola said, sighing heavily. I could see he was

anguishing over what he was about to say next. 'Have you heard from your father?' Nikola had probably been debating all weekend as to how to raise this question with me. Bringing up the topic of fathers was still difficult.

'No, there has been no news. Just updates here and there. You know, rumours that get my hopes up that he will return. He is still in Croatia. I think he was in Bosnia for a while, but now is meant to be up north, along the border. It's strange to imagine that he's actually just hours away from this city … yet it feels like worlds away.'

'You will get him back.' Nikola said this so confidently that I believed him, as though Nikola had some inside news from the frontlines. 'I know that sounds like a stupid thing to say,' he added quickly. 'I know the last thing you need is false hope. But I just have a feeling that your dad will be okay.'

I smiled. 'I'll miss this,' I said to him.

'Me too. But it doesn't have to be the end. You'll be back, I promise you.' Nikola gave me another hug, and we set off for my journey home.

Nikola took me to the train station and carried my small bag the entire way. A few days with my old friend had a therapeutic effect on me. I boarded the train feeling lighter and freer than when I had arrived.

'I'll call you when I make it back to Belgrade!' I called out the window.

Nikola smiled, and all he could yell in return was, '*Selma, ne naginji se kroz prozor!*' I sat back and laughed. *Selma, don't lean out of the window.* Everyone in Yugoslavia knew that line of lyrics. We used to listen to it all the time back at school, Nikola, Ana, Marko and me.

I spent the remainder of the train ride back to Belgrade lost in nostalgic thoughts of not so long ago, in a town not so far away.

Chapter 20

I was woken up by the phone ringing one day, somewhere towards the end of summer in 1993. Those days were all blurred into one. It was the worst phone call I had ever received, and I can't clearly recall most of it. As I picked up the receiver and answered, I heard my Baka Anka say my name in a trembling voice. It was followed by three names, *Branislav*, *Selma* and *Lejla*, and by the word *killed*.

That was all I managed to hear before the ringing in my ears blocked everything else, and my mother walked into the room and saw me, and snatched the phone from my hand, and kept yelling '*What? What?*' and started half-crying and half-screaming, and Alisa came in to try and regain some sense into the both of us, and the phone just lay there forgotten on the ground, my grandmother's crying coming from the other side.

I felt like I was going to be sick, so I just sat down and put my head in my hands. Alisa kept calling out, 'Mama! Mama!' while my mother could only cry out, 'My brother! My brother!'

I remember my mother once saying that sometimes no news was good news, and it was true. The first news our family had received from Sarajevo in quite some time was from a police officer whose job it was to notify immediate family members of the death of loved ones killed by shellfire. Our family was not the only one from their apartment block to perish, he made a point of saying.

When Aunt Dragana entered the room she required no explanation to the scene before her eyes. The screaming, the crying, the phone abandoned on the worn carpet. It brought my aunt collapsing down onto her knees and into a heap, her body trembling from the sobs.

I didn't know who to cry for first.

But the thought of Lejla made me feel a hurt like no other. A furious hurt.

I recalled Uncle Branislav's words to me on the day before I left Sarajevo for the safety of Belgrade. 'You need to leave, even if I cannot,' he had said to me. 'Sarajevo is my home now, because this is where my family is. I'm not going to leave because my wife is Muslim and I'm Orthodox. It's ridiculous. And this is my daughter's city. This will always be her home.'

And as he pulled me into a tight embrace before sending me off on the bus the next night, I barely caught what he said to me in a sharp whisper.

'Mara, get on that bus and get out of here, and don't you ever look back.'

And I couldn't help shake the thought of *it should have been me.* I would have been there with them. I would have died with them. And for a long time after I would still believe that I *should* have died there with them.

But my uncle got me out of Sarajevo and literally saved my life.

Through crystal-eyes I watched my mother and her sister cry into each other's shoulders, and although I knew they cried for their brother, I felt more than anything, they were crying for Selma; they knew there could be no worse pain than that of a mother's after losing her child.

The only consolation being, in this case, that Selma would never know.

At some point I remembered the phone lying on the ground

and went to place it back on the receiver. The dial tone was static when I picked up the phone, but I could still hear my grandmother's heart breaking on the other side, far away, in my hometown that cared nothing for her loss.

I was still in a daze when I saw what had happened to the bridge. The old bridge in Mostar, so old and distinguished, had been reduced to rubble in moments. It felt like yet another personal loss. That was the bridge where Tata had taken me, the bridge of his hometown. It was a magnificent piece of architecture which, for me, symbolised so much more than a bridge. Now, it was a harsh reminder of my father and the uncertainty surrounding his existence.

The day I witnessed the news about the destruction of the old bridge in Mostar, I once again recoiled into a solitary shell, choosing to spend my days in the confines of my room. All I did was play memories in my mind, like a non-sequential video, of those days in my childhood when Tata and I would enter into his past, into Mostar, and remember his Ottoman roots that kept calling him back to the place. He became more forgiving during this time. He suspended his own beliefs and experiences and allowed himself to educate me about each *džamija* he knew of, and the prayers that occurred within. He would regale me with stories of *Suleiman the Magnificent*, and the history of the old bridge and its grandness.

This part of my father only ever revealed itself on rare occasions, and I felt as though it was reserved only for me. For me, my father was willing to relax. He had no one to impress, and deep within him, he had a whole history, an ancestry, which was as much a part of him as any other defining characteristic. When Tata took me to Mostar, it was not only his opportunity to involve me in his heritage—in our *shared* heritage, for his background was also mine—but it was also a time for him to remember his own father. It was in Mostar where Tata had spent much of his childhood, and it was also in Mostar that he lost his father.

When my grandfather Emir died, Tata lost both his father and his hometown. He returned with Baka Roza to the Dalmatia that she knew so well and missed dearly, and it was there that Tata's new sense of belonging evolved. Tata grew into Dalmatia like a butterfly into its wings; it was a natural and effortless process. This land was also a part of him, and the sea of the Adriatic ran through his veins just as much as the waters of the Neretva River. Tata was a man bound to our land through many connections and shared histories, which he passed on to me.

I saw nothing strategic in the destruction of the bridge. I saw no purpose to it, in the same way I saw no purpose to the war. This was a blatant attack on cultural property. To destroy the bridge was to destroy history and memories, and to say without words, 'there is no unity here'. The bridge was a physical and symbolic connection that had been severed. I was mourning more than the loss of a stone structure.

Aunt Dragana worked more than ever, needing to be occupied. My own mother was a shadow, flitting through each room of the apartment like a ghost who haunted it. As winter set in well and truly, our moods collectively took a downward spiral. We avoided the television and all newspapers. We cut ourselves off from the world almost entirely, choosing to be victims of our suffering. We entered a seemingly endless stage of grieving.

The new year came and went, but no one celebrated it. At least not in our home.

One afternoon as I was mindlessly changing my bed sheets, the stack of Marko's letters tumbled out from under my pillow. I picked them up and thought what a stupid place it was to store them; under my pillow, as though a tooth fairy would turn up one night and trade me Marko's letters for the real deal. I put them in my bedside drawer instead.

Looking at the letters, I had a thought. Maybe I could write to Marko. I needed to tell someone about how much I hurt and how I still had nightmares about that day in Sarajevo. I knew Marko would understand. But, when I grabbed a pen and a piece of paper, my mind went blank. I had no idea where to begin and which words to use. I felt completely numb and gave up on the task almost as soon as it had occurred to me.

I dragged myself up and out of the room. *Sorry, Marko. It's all too hard right now.*

My impassivity continued. Each day I would walk my sister to her school and proceed to the university, but when I got there, I was of no use to anyone. I found it beyond difficult to concentrate on anything except my grief. I poured over books and books, but nothing sank in. I forgot to eat, but I didn't feel hungry anyway.

'Mara, do you remember the sound of Tata's voice?'

Alisa had taken me aback with this question. I was walking her to school, bleary-eyed and unfocussed after another restless night. A deceivingly cool wind blew around us, even though autumn had hardly begun.

'Well, yes, I think I do,' I eventually replied to my sister. 'His voice is deep, very masculine. But soft too, not aggressive in any way. It suits him.'

Alisa thought about this and I could see her struggling to materialise the exact sound in her mind.

'I think I'm forgetting ...' she whispered a bit ashamedly. I put my arm around her and brought her close to me, trying to think of a way to comfort her.

'That's perfectly normal,' I reassured my sister. 'We often forget the sound of a person's voice after not having seen them for a while. You know, after a really long time, it's easy to forget all sorts of details about a person; the way they look, the colour of their hair or the way they laugh.'

I still remembered all of these things about Tata though. I couldn't imagine I would ever forget, but I was older than Alisa. I had a lot more memories to draw from.

'Just focus on your best memories of him, okay, Alisa? They're yours to keep.' She smiled to herself and understood, but I could see that Tata's absence was a constant source of worry to her. 'And remember, you could just look in the mirror,' I added. She gave me a quizzical look. 'What I mean is, you have his eyes. And his hair. Your face is almost a reflection of his, you know.'

'Mara,' she said to me once more. 'Is Tata fighting on the good side?'

This question was trickier than her previous one, and I really didn't want to answer it. But my sister was riddled with confusion and I was scared she might be hearing negative comments or opinions elsewhere. I didn't want her to get the wrong idea, but I also needed to protect her memory of our father.

'Alisa, I'm not sure there is a good side,' I finally announced. 'Tata is just doing his job for the same people he has always worked for. You and I both know that he would much rather be doing just about anything else in the world instead of this. Whatever side he is on, remember that he is a good person who would never inflict any unnecessary hurt or suffering upon anyone. He has his principles.'

'Every side thinks they're right, but that's impossible. Someone has to be wrong,' Alisa said. 'Don't they?'

'It may seem like that in movies or books, sure. But, Alisa, you will be amazed at how in reality, an alarming amount of people can all be wrong about the same thing,' I said. I gave her a little grin and didn't say much else. I had to let her form her own opinions.

Alisa stared ahead and nodded in agreement. She was in high school and a bright student, but perhaps still a bit reserved for her age. She kept to herself and was often 'inside her own head' as Mama liked to say. Often her questions were peppered with innocence or immaturity even, and I wondered how confused she must have felt about herself and this world of ours.

And then I thought about how, despite her age, I was still

walking Alisa to school every chance I had. I would convince myself I did it just for the enjoyment of her company, but I knew it was my over-protective nature. If something were to happen to her, I would never forgive myself. But I also had to let her grow up, free of fear and without an overbearing bigger sister watching her like a hawk.

Striding through the hilly streets of Belgrade, I vowed to step back a bit and give my sister some space.

Instead, I refocussed on university and on getting through this final year. It took all the strength I had and all the concentration I could summon, but I became mentally and emotionally tuned out. Every loss, every stab to the heart, every tear shed—I tucked it all away, out of my heart and into the deepest corners of my mind.

Three days before my twenty-fourth birthday, I received a letter.

It was sent from Marko's address in Zadar. His mother had forwarded it onto me, my name written above Aunt Dragana's address. It was the first time I had received any mail here in Belgrade.

I was already preparing myself for some terrible news, having grown accustomed to it the way one grows accustomed to snow during wintertime. I looked upon the familiar scrawl that was Marko's handwriting, recognising it even after all this time had elapsed.

Dear Mara,

Sorry for not having written earlier. How are you? What's new? Stupid questions to ask, I know, considering I can't be sure of where you even are. When I last spoke to my mother she told me you were in Belgrade, so I hope that's still the case.

I'd be surprised if you're still reading my letter by this point. You are probably full of rage and will never forgive me. I understand. I don't deserve forgiveness. But I need you to know that I still think of you and that I have not given up hope for us. Do I sound pathetic, or what? When we were together I hardly ever said how much I loved you, and now here I am putting it all out there like some sad and terrible poet, knowing very well that it could all be too late by now.

I don't want to bore you with details, but things have been hard, to put it mildly. I cannot say what I feel or think at the moment, but I am hoping that one day when I go home, I might be able to sort out this mess in my head. And hopefully that will be soon.

I thought that things were going to start slowing down here, but lately the conflict has been worse than ever. Still, I'm remaining hopeful that the end is near. If all goes well, I'll be able to go home within several months. They keep telling me that but it doesn't seem to happen. It's hard being optimistic. I feel like time has come to a standstill and I have been here, in this same damn uniform, since I can remember.

I don't know what I'm asking of you. You don't need to reply, you don't need to do anything. I am just hopeful that when all this is over, I will still have a friend.

With love,
Marko.

The first thing I felt was relief. Marko was still alive, and he sounded almost … normal? Hopeful? Even apologetic? I had to compose myself. I read the letter multiple times, but I still wasn't sure how to reply to him. I drafted the beginnings of many letters before I thought I should leave it for a day or two and start afresh. I felt those long-forgotten butterflies in my stomach and smiled to myself. I still felt something for him.

Marko with the smiling eyes, whose face was kind.

Marko, who was the funniest boy in school. Marko, the troublemaker in the courtyard. Marko, the athlete, the daredevil, the boy who gifted me books and played me music and loved me in a way no one ever had before.

I loved that Marko. But it meant I also had to love the Marko who never felt good enough, or smart enough, or talented enough. The Marko who was extremely hurt inside and had hurt me too. Was I ready and able to do that?

Yet I clung to the knowledge that he was ok for now, and that tiny flame of hope within me flickered just a little brighter than before.

I rushed home from university on the day of my birthday, since Mama made me promise I would be there for the special lunch and birthday cake she made. I wanted to sit down and finally reply to Marko's letter, but I knew how hard Mama was trying to lift all our spirits and of course I wasn't going to quash that.

I made it to our apartment building just as the postman was delivering the mail.

'Here, I can take that,' I said. He smiled and nodded and handed me the single letter, which wasn't addressed to me, but to Mama. My heart sank a bit. I had almost expected to hear from Marko again.

I took the stairs up to our floor and let myself in.

'*Sretan rodendan!*' My mother, aunt and sister all called out simultaneously as soon as I had entered. I thanked them for the birthday wishes, giving each of them a hug.

'Here Mama,' I said as we made our way to the dining table. 'This just arrived for you.' Mama thanked me and took the letter. Aunt Dragana was spooning food onto all our plates as Alisa went to get some drinks.

'Is mineral water okay or does anyone want something else?' she asked.

'Fine with me,' I replied.

'Me too,' my aunt said.

'Mama?' Alisa asked, looking up at our mother. We all turned to face her. Her expression was frozen. She held the letter with trembling hands whilst the enveloped sat listless beside her feet.

No way. Not again. My immediate thoughts jumped to the worst news imaginable.

'He's coming back,' Mama barely whispered. 'They're releasing him.'

'What?!' Alisa jumped to our mother's side and grabbed the

letter from her. She began to read it and I looked over her shoulder, reading it too.

I couldn't believe it. It was legitimate. The army was finally releasing Tata from his duties.

Aunt Dragana burst into tears, surprising all of us. My mother looked at her and started laughing, loudly. And then she couldn't stop. Her sister paused for a moment, looking confused, until a small smile escaped her. Soon enough, Aunt Dragana was laughing too, until they both had tears in their eyes and had to sit down. Alisa and I exchanged a puzzled look and smiled at each other.

Tata was coming back.

Well, I supposed if this wasn't a reason to laugh with joy, then what was? We took turns reading the letter while we ate our food, laughing and celebrating. When it came time for the birthday cake, my family sang me the birthday song as jubilantly as they would have when I was a child. Then my aunt went to make a few phone calls, letting the rest of our family know. *Tata was safe.*

'So,' Alisa said to me over our second slice of cake. 'Is this the best birthday ever, or what?'

'It most definitely is,' I said to her. It was simply surreal. I hadn't even allowed myself to think about Tata's return very much, so the news consumed me totally. I forgot about everything else. All that pain and loss was suspended for now.

Our world had just been turned upside-down, but the right way around.

Yet amongst everything, Marko's previous letter sat in my bedside drawer with all the others, pushed aside by more pressing news, and waiting for a reply that was not going to come.

Chapter 21

I sat and waited like some loyal pet awaiting its master's return, not daring to move in fear of missing even a glimpse of the one it loved most. I was not going to be convinced of his return until I saw him, safe and whole, standing before me.

The days had been painfully slow since discovering that my father was returning to us. Yet the frustration of waiting did nothing to detract from my gratefulness.

It didn't feel real. The man, my father, had been at the centre of it all; yet he survived, unlike so many other soldiers. There had been those who couldn't have been further removed from the carnage yet still fell victim to it. Was it not the soldier who was meant to be the first to go? The almost definite loss? He was a willing participant, well, as willing a participant as one could be in such circumstances. But fate, or whatever it was, had spared him. Not fate; luck. How lucky he was to have made it. How guilty I felt, to know that I wouldn't have him trade his place for even the most innocent of victims.

Not even the gargoyles atop Notre Dame were as still as I was that day, counting down the hours on the steps of our apartment building.

And, when the taxi drove up into the gravel parking lot in front of our building, and the tall, solid figure of my father stepped out from the passenger side, I physically felt my shoulders loosen and the tension in my neck release itself.

My heartbeat began working overtime, excited, nervous, expectant and elated. My emotions didn't know how to handle themselves but in a physical translation, through increasing breathing and beating and sweating and rapid blinking and gentle trembling.

He turned, looking up at the new home awaiting him, a tower of mediocrity and uniformity. He looked back down, at the dusty ground beneath him. I barely whispered, 'Tata,' and he looked up to see me, a lone figure on the dirty apartment building steps.

'*Ljubav moja*,' I heard him say in a strained voice, more to himself than to me. *My love*. And the sound of his voice was familiar once more, as though it had always been there all these years, speaking straight into my ear.

Neither of us ran, but we walked slowly towards each other, until in a sudden and quick movement we both grabbed the other, holding on tight in an embrace I had thought I would never feel again. I was in Tata's arms, where I had always felt safest. In that moment, I was a young child again. I was crying, too, like a child, so indescribably happy to see my father, so desperate to tell him everything. I simply yearned for his words to enter my ears and to make me feel as though everything would be okay once more.

Holy shit, I thought to myself. He could have died. He could have so easily been gone forever, but he remained alive throughout it all. I started to laugh, and so did he. We both laughed, like two crazy people suddenly aware of just how damn lucky they were.

My father then grabbed my face in his hands and stared straight into my eyes. He shook his head and told me everything he had to say in that one look. I touched his face and told him everything too. There were no anxious feelings, no awkwardness between us. Around my father, I was as I had always been—so showered with love and so full of love for him, that I was positively invincible.

I led him upstairs to our apartment, holding his hand the entire way.

I only let go of it when he saw Mama and Alisa, and then finally, did he start to cry. And he looked so beautiful to me in that moment.

Each one of us had journeyed so far just to be here, where we had wanted to be all along—with each other. And right now, it didn't matter *where* that place was, because we had a home again.

As happy as I was for my sister and I to have our father back, I was utterly relieved for my mother. She looked as though she had spent the last few years spinning in a tumble dryer and was finally now able to stop and get out; she was like someone who had just run a marathon and greeted the finish line with the purest sense of longing and joy. At the sight of my father, her world had stopped spinning haphazardly and was able to stabilise.

None of us would leave his side for some time, and Tata was relishing each moment. What I had expected from his return was a hollow man, with destruction in his eyes and a body trembling with trauma. But the man who came back appeared to be my same father. I noticed small changes in the way he spoke more quietly and less often, and certain things he didn't speak of at all. He spent more time looking at us, at my mother, Alisa and me. He hardly left the apartment.

In seeing him, though, another face appeared in my mind, as though it were the missing piece of the whole puzzle: the face of Marko. Whatever state of paralysis I had been in was starting to dissipate, and the urge to see and hear from Marko began to rise in me. I wanted to feel that relief. I wanted to jump into Marko's arms the way I had jumped into Tata's arms. I wanted to think we could continue, peacefully, as we had done before.

But I was only kidding myself if I thought that things would ever be the same again. It was time to find a 'new' normal.

Nobody spoke about Zadar. We all knew we couldn't return to our hometown and expect to get our lives back. Yet it was like a member of the family was still missing and we couldn't really function as a whole. Zadar had been like the chess board on which we all moved around on, clearly knowing which way to go, and how, and why. In Belgrade, it was like playing checkers; sometimes we moved together and other times we jumped over one another, not sure of the space or how to use it.

We treaded gently around each other's sensitivities, spoke little of the atrocities, and did our best to slowly put pieces of our lives back in order. But sometimes the things left unsaid were too unbearable.

I was helping Mama fold the laundry one evening when I suddenly thought to ask her. 'Mama,' I said. 'Was it ever real, everything we had? Was it as good as we believed it to be?' As though we were carrying on from an earlier conversation only moments ago, my mother knew exactly what I was talking about.

'I don't know, dear,' she said to me. 'No, it wasn't real. But we believed it all anyway. Who wouldn't want to live thinking they had everything? It was a beautiful illusion, that's what it was.'

I felt slightly robbed, as though I had been lied to. I had grown up believing in something amazing and indestructible, only to realise it was all a fairy-tale. I had believed in our system just as much as my mother had, yet she accepted its disappearance. Maybe my mother had known all along that it was too idealistic to have been real, but I never thought such a thing. I was convinced that it *was* the real thing, that we *did* have something wonderful in this country of ours. Why had no one ever told me otherwise? Why did they allow me to go on believing in something so fragile? How could they?

I was overcome by a feeling of betrayal, like our entire lives had all been an elaborate set-up. I knew my mother was just as shattered as I was, but she had given me an answer I didn't want to hear. Surely my father couldn't be so ambivalent about it. He would tell me that it had all been perfectly real and amazing, and that it was the usual enemies of fascism, capitalism and religion that were responsible for our destruction.

'Do you even care?' I said to my mother. She gave me a puzzled look. 'That we lost it all, I mean. Do you even care, if it was all fake to you anyway?'

I knew immediately that I had badly overstepped my limits. I never spoke down to my mother, and I was already preparing myself for her wrath. But it didn't come.

I looked at my mother and saw her downcast gaze and trembling lips. She wasn't angry at me. She was too upset to be mad.

'Mama, I'm sorry. I didn't mean to say it like that,' I said.

She shook her head to say it wasn't my fault. She composed herself and looked up at me, straight into my eyes.

Clinging tightly to the newly-washed singlet in her hands, she said to me, 'I'm so sorry we filled your mind with such strong convictions. But we did it so that you would grow up to be a good person, free from hatred and full of hope ... even if it was hope for an impossibly ideal existence.'

I looked away from her, feeling guilty.

'But most of all,' my mother continued, firmly now. 'I'm sorry that your hope fell apart before your eyes, and I did nothing to prepare you for its loss.'

I was left feeling empty. My mother had a purpose all along. Her dedication to our home country and its ideologies was not out of a trivial sense of patriotism, but out of a desire to see those values passed on to future generations. She wanted to give me something worthwhile to believe in. Otherwise, she risked losing me to the deep-rooted hate and fear that lay beneath the surface of our *brotherhood and unity*. For her, the illusion was extremely important, no matter the pretence.

'Mama,' I said to her. 'It was real for me. I believed in it. And I still have hope.'

She smiled at me feebly, but with a hint of happiness.

'You know, Mara ... I believed in it, too.'

The news still reminded us each day of what couldn't be ignored. It told us of even greater horrors than anything I had seen or heard— of massacres and entire annihilations of people and towns. What viciousness humans were capable of, was something I was still learning. Even my father received moments of shock and disgust at what was being revealed. It appeared as though only now were we beginning to find out just what we had done to ourselves as a people.

Bit by bit, pieces of information came together, but even then, it was all selective. Trust had been abolished, and the details were always murky. I took it all in with a good amount of scepticism. Eventually, I failed to see the point of it all. The television was turned off in favour of books and music, and I began to slowly rediscover those simple pleasures that had once belonged in my life.

So, we carried on, watching things settle as the war in Yugoslavia became resigned to the history books. Our people were exhausted and needed a rest. And there would be many long months ahead, years even, for damaged families still waiting to identify lost loved ones and to lay them to rest.

But jumping back onto your feet, for millions of people at once, is as difficult as it sounds. I had not yet found a job after finishing university, and it only added to my sense of displacement. But my father was proud nonetheless.

'My Mileva, a scientist,' he would say. 'You've lived up to your namesake.'

'Well I'm not quite a physicist like Mileva Marić was. Biology was my major—'

'A-a-a,' my father would interrupt. 'As noble a science as any. I know you'll be amazing.'

I hoped so, too.

Collectively, we turned to Mama for hope and stability. Aunt Dragana assisted her to find a job in a bank. Nothing glamorous, but generous enough that we were finally able to move out and get a place of our own. My family of four relocated somewhere quieter, to a small apartment across the river. My mother was happiest of all, now that she had earned back a sense of independence. Things were slowly starting to look like what they once had.

Naturally, there still remained signs of a disrupted family. I spent most of my time with the sister I was still getting to know, offering her half-hearted words of optimism for the future. My mother attempted to over-compensate by being the perfect wife, mother and worker. She was carrying all our burdens. My father didn't have a work to return to; his army no longer existed. He tried to make himself useful, but clearly needed time to adjust. And despite knowing he had arrived in a city that wouldn't condemn him for his past, he couldn't help but miss our true home.

As he said, 'Nothing could ever replace the Adriatic, not even the grand Danube.'

With all the preparation I had had to adjust to shocks, to surprises, to terror, to the unthinkable, to the devastating, to the potential of human evil, I found myself decidedly *unprepared* for one event.

The return of Marko.

I would be lying if I said I had not thought of him intensely during the last few months, imagined him engaged in combat somewhere, longed for him in moments of desperation. I felt pangs of guilt at times, knowing that I was still somehow functioning within my sense of normality, yet he had likely experienced the worst the war had to offer, upfront and in detail. I had to remind myself countless times that these were the choices he and I made; he, to go to war, and I, to escape it. And I had to remember what he was representing, after all. *Everything that I was not.*

I still hadn't responded to the one letter he had sent me. At first, the news of Tata's return overshadowed everything. Yet when Tata did return and the excitement settled, I was taken aback by how Tata's presence made Marko's betrayal feel all the more intense. It bred a level of resentment in me that lasted long enough for me to forget why I had been so angry in the first place, but I managed to hold onto my grudge nonetheless. Every time I felt like yielding to temptation and contacting Marko, I reminded myself that I was still too hurt. I had to 'let it go'. My loyalty towards my father had clouded all other feelings.

But my reminders grew weaker and weaker, and eventually even the hurt lessened and gave way to more powerful feelings of longing yet again. And I was sure there had to be an explanation for it all.

It was from my Baka Roza that I learned about Marko's family. Her phone calls had become more regular since Tata's return, but it was mostly her son she spoke to. Yet Baka Roza's love for small town gossip had not fluctuated during all these years, and she called to tell me she had heard certain whisperings and rumours and had gone to investigate the whereabouts of my old friend. Her actions left me feeling humbled for she knew how much Marko meant to me.

'The Ivanić family have recently relocated to another part of town, to an apartment on the half-island. While everyone else was struggling to make ends meet during the last few years, Marko's family have somehow profited,' Baka Roza told me, unforgivingly. 'Your guess is as good as mine as to where their money came from ... but that's another one of those things that does not get talked about, at least not yet. Neither does anyone mention their reclaimed property in *Borik*, or the new car his father just purchased: a Mercedes. Who the hell is buying a Mercedes in Croatia right now?!'

Baka Roza, as cynical and suspicious as always—that's what I would have once thought. But Baka Roza's intuition had never been wrong. Whilst keeping a low profile in Zadar all this time, she observed all the changes as keenly as a lioness on the prowl.

But I knew that Marko was not his father. I was almost certain he wasn't living it up in penthouse apartments and beachside getaways at the expense of others.

'Thanks, Baka,' I replied. 'And please, if you see Marko, at least let him know how I am. Nothing else.'

'Of course, Mara.'

I waited for the phone to ring each day, but quickly grew disenchanted.

His voice came in the form of another letter. But this one, I chose not to put away.

Short and to the point, Marko had obtained my new address and written me the briefest of letters. He wanted to know the necessaries first: how I was and where I was living. My reply was also short, immediately demanding information from him. I couldn't help but notice his letters appeared void of any emotion, never straying into explicit details or feelings.

Eventually I got a letter from him saying that he was not sure how much longer he could keep writing to me—his parents were sure to find out eventually, and they strongly disapproved of Marko and I having any sort of contact. By 'his parents', I knew he really meant his father. When I suggested he find an alternate address, or simply *call me* when he knew he was alone, he made excuses: *I cannot trust anyone else to receive your letters; I cannot be seen going to your family's home to pick up mail; I am not ready yet for you to hear my voice; my parents will see the record of phone calls coming from Serbia ...*

I knew Marko was evading something. Perhaps he feared confrontation? In a bout of frustration, I sent him another letter demanding some truth and sincerity. I told him I missed him, that I didn't want to bring up the past, but rather, I wanted to know of our future. I told him how I managed to overcome all the resentment and grief, how I *could not* just let it go, and that it took me a long time to get to this point. I sent the letter, a stream of emotions and thoughts, and feared the response I would get, if I were to get one at all.

It was many weeks later when I finally received one in return. It was a miserable day in Belgrade as I sat in my room with the envelope in my hands, preparing myself for its contents.

He sounded frantic. His sentences were fragmented, nonsensical. The letter was, in essence, a series of pleas and cries for help. *You need to come back*, was repeated several times. *I need to see you, this isn't right*. I had thought he was becoming distant, but now he appeared anxious and afraid of the space between us.

I didn't know how to reply. Two days had passed since I received another such letter. It was very similar in content, begging me to return home to see him. Short. Desperate.

Whatever emotion was lacking previously was being made up for now. However, it was not an emotion that stemmed from a growing fondness in his heart; rather, it was coming from a dark space in his head. I began to grow concerned. In my mind, preparations were already underway to return to Zadar. Not because I wanted to, but because my best friend needed me.

For him, I would return.

Chapter 22

Few people were travelling from Serbia to Croatia. The bus clamoured along the unkempt and hole-ridden roads of what was once Yugoslavia, ensuring its passengers felt every imperfection of the surface beneath them. I thought about the last time I took this journey, although travelling in the opposite direction.

The passengers did not appear to have changed. It was always the same combination of mostly elderly people. Where they were going and for what reasons, I never knew. They looked as though they didn't care anymore; that whatever tensions arose at the border control or whatever fear might be felt upon crossing into unwelcome territory, it was all meaningless. Too much effort, too much of life spent in unhappiness. Nothing left to lose anyway. I received a few sideways glances from my companions on the bus but gave nothing in return.

In my last letter to Marko, sent weeks ago, I had promised him I would come to Zadar as soon as possible. I didn't give him an exact date, which was really due to my own uncertainty. I knew I had a lot of convincing to do, that I would meet a lot of resistance from my parents. Mama was worried, apprehensive and naturally opposed to it. But Tata seemed to understand just by looking at me.

'Go,' he had said. 'Go back home. Your friend is waiting for you.'

So, I left the next day, figuring I had wasted enough time as it was. With only the inconsistent letter-writing to go by, coupled with his fragile mindset, I feared that Marko might not be expecting me at all.

But I had, of course, been able to inform my grandparents. And as reliable as always, Baka Anka and Dida Ilija were already waiting for me. Throughout the bus ride into Croatia, I acted like a horse wearing blinders; I stared only straight ahead, fearful of getting spooked by something I might see through the corner of my eye. It wasn't until the bus clumsily rolled into the station that I dared look around. There were very few of us but I was still the last one to get off the bus. I took a deep breath, as I imagine Neil Armstrong would have, right before taking a step into something he'd spent so long fantasising about.

'*Oko moje!*' Dida Ilija's voice carried across to where I was standing.

Upon seeing them I forgot my initial reason for returning, for I only had eyes for my grandparents. There they were, these survivors of wars. These savers of lives.

I was gliding across the ground, my soles attuned to the earth of the Adriatic coastline. I moved slowly towards my grandparents with a lump in my throat the size of a small bird. Holding out my arms, I embraced them both, my Baka and Dida. I pushed my face into their shoulders so they wouldn't see me cry, and I could hear Baka Anka whispering *our girl, our girl, our girl*. We held each other for some time before I let go and let Dida take my hand in his own, as we walked towards the car to make the familiar journey back to my former apartment, back to the home where I had grown up, alongside the boy I grew up with.

Baka Anka had changed somehow; she had become more capable and fierce. When we arrived at the car that once belonged to my parents, she immediately sat in the driver's seat, as confident as a Formula One race car driver. I knew my grandmother could drive, I had just never really *seen* her do it. But I suppose she had to, being the only one able to do so. Living comfortably in Lika, she sometimes drove Dida to the local doctor's, but never further. Everyone always came to her, usually. So, I accepted this new sight and thought admirably of my Baka Anka, who charmed me with her chameleon-like adaptability.

Baka Anka chatted with me as though only days had passed since our last meeting. I knew she was trying hard to make this comfortable for me, to go back to our old ways. And it was working, despite my obvious distracted tone. I couldn't help looking out of the window, taking in every square inch of the city, attempting to spy changes along the way. Dida Ilija smiled at me and kept leaning back to squeeze my hand, and I smiled back at him. I suppose as long as I was with my family, then things could feel normal.

Arriving home, however, was not. We pulled into the courtyard and a sense of unease crept up on me. There was no Marko waiting, and I looked in the direction of his former apartment. The windows had new curtains in them, belonging to a new family inside. There were many new cars in the parking lot, making it clear that a large reshuffling had occurred. Out with the old, in with the new.

I climbed up the stairs, following my grandparents. A familiar smell filled my nostrils when we entered our apartment. My breath quivered as I let out a long sigh, overwhelmed by a flood of memories. My room, the kitchen, the TV in the living room where so many basketball games had been watched. The balcony, where we sat and ate watermelon to ease the heat of summer months. Too many thoughts were invading my mind and impairing my ability to remain calm and in control. *Holy shit*, I thought to myself. *Did the past few years actually happen?*

A brief wave of panic washed over me, and I hated that I was still dealing with the shock of what had happened. It was a loss I would never get over. There would always be moments in the future where I would be caught out, unsuspecting, and my disbelief at the harsh reality of it all would yet again take over my mind. *This is not fair*, was all I could think. *This is meant to be my home.*

I took a breath to steady myself and thought, *this is nothing compared to what it will be like to see Marko*. I had to be stronger.

I sat down at the kitchen table where a feast awaited me. Lunch with my grandparents, lovingly cooked by Baka. This was something I had missed the most. Not just for the food (although that was incredibly important, too) but for what it meant. I began to relax. As we ate our meals, I allowed myself to revel in this favourite pastime of mine.

Dida Ilija and I couldn't take our eyes off each other as we ate, while Baka Anka spoke to Baka Roza over the phone, informing her that I was safe and well, promising her she would be able to see me soon.

I had no clear plan of what to do first. I thought I would make my way to Marko's place, but my grandmother advised me against it.

'Not today, at least. It is too much for you. Have some rest and go tomorrow.'

I agreed, relieved to be able to excuse myself from any more action for the day. *The morning is smarter than the night*, Tata would always tell me. Tomorrow then, I would be smarter and my brain clearer. Tomorrow, I would go and repair all that was broken.

I awoke the next morning feeling somewhat surprised by how well-rested I was. It was as though my body had recognised my comfy bed in my old bedroom. Midday approached by the time I actually got out of my room, which I was reluctant to leave, and made my way into the kitchen. Baka was already making lunch and Dida was shelling walnuts on the balcony.

'Good morning, Mara,' my grandmother said. 'Have something to eat. And you might want to check the mail, there is a letter for you. It might have been in the mailbox for a few days by the looks of it.'

'Thanks, I will,' I said. I wondered how many people still thought I lived here and were trying to contact me. Surely not too many.

I stepped into the hallway and spotted the letter addressed to me sitting by the phone. I picked it up hurriedly, recognising Marko's writing. But unlike the other letters from him, this one had no stamp and no return address. Maybe he was anticipating my return and didn't know where to send the letter to? Had we somehow missed each other, like ships in the night?

'Baka Anka!' I called out. 'Did someone personally drop off this letter?'

'Well they must have!' she called back. 'Even though it was in the mailbox, it had no stamp or anything!'

So, Marko *must* have been here. But that's weird. Didn't he know I was coming to Zadar? Wouldn't he have checked to see if I was here?

I went back into my room with the letter, unfolding it to reveal Marko's wobbly handwriting.

Dearest Mara,

I hope this letter receives you. I know that asking you to come back to Zadar was too much and it's fair of you to ignore me. I'm sorry for doing that to you. And I know that even if I was to see you, you would find a way to convince me to change my mind. And I don't want that, either.

I know what I am about to do will hurt many people and that you especially will not approve, but I see no other way out. I do not want to see, or hear, or feel anything.

I killed a man, Mara. In cold blood. This was on top of the bombings, the shooting and the general carnage we were responsible for. I know it is no excuse to say, 'they made me do it', but they did. Like some sort of sick test of manhood, I was told to point the gun at his head and pull the trigger. He was just an old man, no threat to anyone or anything. But he was a Serb, and that made it justifiable. All I could think about was you. Imagine if that was you. I couldn't have done it then. But somehow I did it. I didn't know him, so I did it.

I don't know what I was thinking, joining this war. I don't know who or what I was fighting for. They fed us all the usual stories about independence and freedom, but I just never felt that strongly about it. You know me—when did I ever give a shit about politics? For me, everything was going fine just the way it was. I think I was trying to convince myself more than anyone else ... that maybe I could be someone.

Mara, I can say sorry a million times over to the people I've killed and hurt, to the families that have suffered, and it wouldn't be enough. Yet my biggest regret is what I did to us. I hope you'll find a way to forgive me. But whatever anyone says, I don't think we are different people. You and I are best friends who grew up together, who loved each other, and nothing can change that.

You are the best thing I had in all my life and I managed to mess it up. And without love... what else is there? I have already seen hell on earth. Whatever comes next has to be better than this.

Please read the story I have enclosed for you. You might recognise it ... and it explains things better than I ever could. Books are pretty amazing, as it turns out.

Love,

Marko.

My mind was a mess, trying to make sense of what Marko was implying. *I know what I am about to do will hurt many people and that you especially will not approve, but I see no other way out.* What did that mean? And why did he think I was ignoring him? Starting to panic, I looked down at the several sheets of paper that had also been in the envelope. I couldn't understand why he'd send me a story. He outwardly expressed a lack of interest in reading, but perhaps that was all an act. Had he changed so much? Is this something that had developed during our separation?

I looked down at the title, *A Perfect Day for Bananafish*. The name sounded familiar, but I was sure I'd never read it. Then I looked down at the author: J.D. Salinger. *My God*. It was the first story. The first story from Salinger's *Nine Stories*, torn straight out of the book. The first and last thing I ever gave to Marko.

It was the story of a soldier. A soldier in a new world. A soldier with scars and wounds that wouldn't go away, until he did.

I proceeded to read it.

When I got to the end, Marko's words finally made sense to me. I dropped the story he so kindly had me read, each sheet of paper listlessly falling onto my bedspread. That final sentence was all too clear:

Then he went over and sat down on the unoccupied twin bed, looked at the girl, and fired a bullet through his right temple.

I put my head in my hands, and I couldn't move. I wasn't aware of it, but I was breathing rapidly and rocking back and forth. That was how my grandmother found me when she walked into my room to announce that lunch was ready.

On my bed with my head in my hands, crying for the loss of a boy with smiling eyes, whose face was kind.

I began to walk. I walked full of purpose but thinking about nothing, all the way to the city. I continued on across the narrow streets, through the park, Vruljice, and along the marina where the *Barka* offered rides to the other side. I strolled mindlessly past the young families with children. Zadar was emanating its Adriatic glow, carrying on being beautiful in spite of all the ugliness that had occurred within it.

As I walked across the bridge towards Poluotok, I took in the view before me. The marina, with its boats of varying shapes and conditions gently rocking on the still water; the church tower of Sveti Donat, reaching over the rooftops of the centre, like the mast of a ship; and the stoned, wall façade of the city's entrance, growing larger as I approached it.

Some things never do change.

Upon crossing the bridge and heading into the centre of town, I didn't turn right at the Kalelarga as I usually might, but took a left turn, heading away from the main square and the Riva. I was alone as I zigzagged through the cobbled alleyways, only the flutter of a bird's wings to break the silence every so often. It didn't take me long to find Marko's new address, and to look up at the top floor of the building before me, knowing it was all taken up by his family. I presumed they had not abandoned their newfound extravagance after the loss of their only son.

He had been my first friend, my first love, my only companion. I felt angry at myself for not thinking of him more often and more deeply, even for daring to hate him for the decisions he had made. I never stopped loving him.

I rang the doorbell to the apartment block in a sudden motion, making sure to do so quickly. I didn't want to get cold feet at this point. Nobody answered, so I tried to push open the door gently. It worked, and I let myself inside. The steps before me were obviously old, but still majestic. They were not the concrete steps with peeling, metal banisters of the apartment blocks I had grown used to. These steps were made of stone, and a polished, wooden banister allowed my hand to glide over it as I climbed each step. I was entering a place of a time before socialism, in a post-socialist society. Once more, I contemplated for a moment the winds of change that blew around Zadar, yet left parts of the city preserved.

I had reached a large, wooden door on the third and final storey. I knocked weakly and waited. I wondered whether I had knocked loud enough for no one was answering. In fact, I had no way of knowing if anyone was even home. I knocked once more, a bit louder this time, but still nothing. I was amazed to realise that of all things that could go wrong and that I had pre-emptively prepared for, 'nobody being home' wasn't one of those things. I tried one last time, knocking loudly, louder than I had intended, the echoes carrying down through the building.

The door was opened violently by a large man, who was yelling at me to be quiet. Then Marko's father realised he was looking at me, and I at him. His eyes were watery and he looked haggard. The gold cross hanging from his neck was shimmering in the light, almost as if it were showing off. It was tangled in his chest hairs, and I found it absurdly crude and unsightly for some reason. We stood in silence, and then a woman suddenly appeared. It was Marko's mother.

She started wailing and her husband just stood there. He had a look of utter hatred on his face. He knew what I was and he couldn't get past it. His loathing went straight through me, saying more than words ever could.

'You need to leave,' he told me.

'Did he get my letter?!' I demanded. 'Did he know I was coming back?'

'Some nerve you had, writing letters to this address,' Marko's father hissed. My mouth dropped open as the realisation hit me. He knew about my letter.

'You think you could just return? We made it perfectly clear that you, and everyone like you, is not wanted here,' he continued. 'You've *never* been wanted here.'

He saw my letter. He saw it, and he made sure that Marko never would.

'Do you … have any idea … what you've done?' I stuttered.

I turned to leave, my mind numb. I was starting to question why I had ever made my way to this place. What was I looking for? Closure? Peace of mind? Or was I expecting Marko to suddenly appear at the doorway, laughing because everything was just a big charade?

Marko's father was about to say something else but I had already turned away, too stunned to argue. There would have been no point.

My legs weakly carried me down the stairs to the echoes of

Marko's mother's cries, which became muffled after their front door slammed shut. I staggered into the warm sunlight outside, gasping for air and not knowing where to go or what to think.

I heard the door open behind me and saw Marko's mother once again. She had run downstairs to see me. She came up to me and held my hands. I tried not to show my shock at the sight of her shrunken frame. She was skeletal.

'His father says that what he did was a sin ... there will be a private funeral, but it will not be spoken about. Please do not come here again. I do not want you exposed to my husband. I do not want you to remember us like this,' she said, her voice giving way to sobs.

My bottom lip was trembling and tears were streaming down my face. I couldn't bring myself to thank this woman who saw me for what I was. She looked at me and shook her head, and I knew that whatever she may have felt before, about this entire war, she now felt that nothing was worth it. She had lost her only son because of the darkness that had taken over him. I nodded to her, squeezed her hands and turned to go.

She grabbed me quickly, taking a surprisingly strong hold of my arm. 'He loved you so much ...' she trailed off.

I pulled away, unable to bear it anymore. I turned and fled. Away from Marko's family and the sight of suffering.

Marko had done it. Robbed himself of his life. Shot himself in the head—his beautiful head with that beautiful face—with a gun that had no doubt felt all too familiar in his hands.

I walked once more through the city, but this time I didn't go back across the bridge. I stayed on Poluotok and ran straight to the Riva, where I stopped by the edge of the platform, where the land meets the sea. I stopped only to look up at the islands and the sky before me, and then I screamed. I screamed so loudly, my voice was like water pouring out of a bucket.

People around me backed away awkwardly, fearing the crazy young woman by the sea. I didn't care. I stood motionless and whimpering, but mostly outraged.

I collapsed in a weak and pathetic heap on the ground, where the salty scent of the sea water below me mixed with the salty taste of my tears, as though they were one, as though by crying I was filling up the Adriatic with my tears.

With great strength, I managed to catch my breath and stopped crying long enough to look up, in an attempt to clear my aching thoughts. Sitting by the Riva, I knew what I had heard was a lie. I *am* wanted here. I *do* belong here. I spent my childhood here; one where all the children played in the courtyard and where we all watched over each other. I longed for the days where no one looked at me as though I was something lesser. I longed for the days where Marko looked at me like he could love no one else, and never would.

Love me in a way like you have never loved before.

I looked out towards the islands and began to cry again, heavily now, thinking about the time spent with my best friend, the boy with smiling eyes, whose face was kind.

His name was Marko, and I loved him.

Several days had passed since the incident. That's what I called it now: the 'incident'. That final letter, that story, that *ending* to the story, was still fresh in my mind. The funeral had come and gone, which I only knew about from the short obituary placed in the newspaper. I had not been invited, naturally. I was not present for my best friend's funeral. I was not there to make sure that they played good music to see him off, just as I promised I would do, all those years ago.

At first, I was too paralysed by my own grief, but it quickly gave way to a crippling sense of guilt. Marko's death was my fault. *If only* I had come back to Zadar sooner. *If only* I had gone to him immediately. *If only* I had known, I would have stopped him from doing it.

And if only *he* had known that I had never forgotten him, then things would have been different. I had to believe that things would have been different.

But to think that he could have died believing I no longer loved him—that was too devastating of a notion for me to dwell on.

There were so many things to be angry about. Unexpectedly, I was angered by the lack of talking. How foreign, I thought, of this town and these people, that there be no rumours circulating among the neighbours, no hushed conversations and gossip exchanged. How *dare* they. There was no sign anywhere that my best friend had killed himself. There was no sign that a young man had been on this Earth and left it. Life went on without him, no utterance of his departure apart from the mouths of those who knew. It felt so terribly unfair.

I was lying in my old bedroom, staring at nothing in particular, when my Dida Ilija entered. He came and sat at the foot of my bed and offered me a smile. I took it and gave him one in return. I realised that this man was smiling, despite having lost his home, his son, despite having lost too much for any single person to bear in one lifetime. Lika had been rid of Serbs, and our property there was now in someone else's hands. Dida's life had been uprooted at an age when it should have been winding down, yet he stood his ground.

'*Oko moje*,' he said to me. 'Sometimes I think my deafness is a blessing, for it has meant that I have heard nothing of the hatred that has been spoken these past few years. Maybe that is why I have no hatred myself? But who knows? I see you, and you have experienced too much for someone so young ... I ask only that you not let hate consume you.'

I nodded.

'You know, during World War Two, your grandmother and I were placed in a concentration camp for some time. *Jasenovac*. The Ustashe were in charge, and they especially cruel in their methods, to say the least. But there was one man, a rich and influential man, who made special provisions to take me out of the camp each day in order to work on his nearby property. He valued my knowledge of agriculture, and, of course, my strength. I would plough his fields, harvest his produce, toil away all day long. But it meant that I was not in the camp. At the end of each day, he would give me whatever meat he had left over and some cheese if I was lucky. But I would refuse it, and I asked that he go and hand it to my Anka instead, in her part of the camp. And he did. This man was my only contact with her.'

Dida paused, thinking about what he wanted to say.

'This man,' he continued, 'was Croatian. He was also very right-wing. And you know what? After some time, he grew so fond of me, that he helped me and your grandmother escape that camp and survive the war. He got to know me as a person, as a *human*, and that changed everything. Now what I am trying to tell you, is that there is good and evil everywhere. I have never felt any hatred towards anyone, even after everything that has happened to me and my family. How could I? I saw terrible things, but I also saw the good in people. In this country, we have always lived side by side, for as long as I can remember, and even longer. We people here in the Balkans, we are forever bound to one another, whether through love or hate. But do not judge. Do not make the unfortunate mistake of thinking we think and act like a group, rather than as individuals. People are complex beings, and change is always possible. Always look at the individual, *oko moje.*'

I squeezed his hand, and mouthed to him, 'Of course, Dida.'

He got up and left my room, leaving me to my thoughts. Dida was magical. He always knew, even without me saying anything. He knew of the fears I had, and of the hatred that was brewing. But he managed to stifle it. I would not disappoint my family by becoming my own worst enemy. I would abandon any feelings of hatred, however raw my wounds, and I would no longer look to blame anyone. There was nothing to gain from it, after all.

It was time to leave, for there always had to come a time to leave. Life went on—mine did, at least—and I had to move on with it. Whatever course it was to take, it was not going to take place here.

It would be a long time before I would feel all right about returning here. The all too familiar ritual of packing and saying goodbye began once more, but where emotion was usually brewing, I felt nothing but a void. A giant, gaping hole had opened up within me and nothing would ever be able to fill it.

I would carry that cavernous, empty well within me for as long as I lived, for it is the place that was reserved for someone who was no longer with me.

I studied my desk, still here, in the room Alisa and I once shared. We used to have so many things arranged on this desk, from overlapping homework papers, to comic books and discarded lolly wrappers. It never once felt cramped. My high school graduation photo was still stuck up on the wall above the desk. I didn't put it there, so I presume Alisa must have. She must have looked at it every day while I was gone.

I still had my sister. I still had my parents. I had so many people, in fact, who made my life worth living. And I had myself, and I knew even that was enough.

Marko's last letter and Salinger's story were sitting in a pile on the centre of my desk. I hesitated, then took the sheets of paper with me. I examined each bit of paper, looking for maybe a fingerprint or a stain of some sort. I sniffed the ink on the page, and almost for a moment, I swore I could smell Marko's skin. I closed my eyes and pictured him here, feeling surprisingly content when I opened them again.

I couldn't save Marko. I never could have.

I let out a heavy sigh and took one final look around. *Time to go home*, I thought.

I quietly exchanged goodbyes with my grandmothers, both of whom were here watching me leave, yet again. They still fussed over me and told me to take care, to eat well and to dress warm. There was a new connection formed between us now. A shared understanding of loss, and shared knowledge that the price we pay for love, is grief. But these resilient women showed me that I would be ok, too. I was a Balkan woman, after all, and capable of enduring so much.

My grandmothers tearfully bid me goodbye once more, as I followed my Dida Ilija out the door for one long and final walk out of Zadar.

My feet walked me through the echoing hallways and down the stairs, out into the open courtyard below our apartment. Dida was a few paces ahead of me, and as he walked, I thought about all the times I had traced these exact same steps on my way to town. It wasn't so unbearable. My senses still took in that familiar smell of an approaching summer heat, the soft touch of the sun on my skin, the sound of crackling pine trees in the warmth.

It was the feeling of Dalmatia.

I felt it all around me, as though it were resurfacing. It was always a part of me, and I a part of it. There, somewhere deep inside of me, I could feel the voice of my city, begging me for forgiveness. And I knew, one day, I would be ready to accept it.

Epilogue

Belgrade's streets kept me sheltered, giving me a purpose and serving as a guide. On these streets, nobody bothered me and nobody knew me. I spent hours exploring them, observing them and leaving my mark on them with each footstep. Belgrade offered something new each day, if I went far enough and if I was open-minded enough. When I felt the anxiety coming on, I would wander these streets.

Which is where I am now.

I felt as though I had to go to the old part of town today, away from the commotion and closer to the river. I walked from the bus stop all the way up to the fortress, where I could watch the Danube on its course, never stopping. It was only then that I started to feel better, to calm down and empty my mind. I channelled all my thoughts onto the river and it took them away from me, downstream and forgotten.

I decided to head towards Skadarlija today; it drew me in just like Baščaršija once had. I needed to see this part of the city, a break from the dark and towering buildings that dominate so much of Belgrade. I wanted to feel the city at its most beautiful, to walk the streets where poets once walked and to know that wondrous minds once inhabited the same space I do.

I strolled gently onto Skadarska street, which appeared before me like an old friend you're always happy to see. I already knew each bar, restaurant and café on this street, so I went further. I found a side street with a small café and sat outside in the afternoon sun. Skadarska street was packed with people today. I didn't mind; I liked seeing all the couples, the families, the young and old.

I took out a book out from my shoulder bag, one I almost always carried with me but had not read in a long time: J.D. Salinger's *Nine Stories*.

I only wanted to read one story.

I picked up the book and opened it to the start of *A Perfect Day for Bananafish*.

A waiter arrived and asked me what I would like to drink. I answered him, hardly looking up. '*Cockta*, please.'

'Ah, the drink of our youth,' I heard him say as he walked away. I smiled a little. *Cockta* has been the drink of our youth for so long that the youths who originally drank it could now be found mostly in retirement homes. I was glad that I was still drinking it. I thought that maybe if I continued to retain some habits from my younger days, to do things that Marko once enjoyed doing too, then he was not totally gone. I would be fondly reminded of him in times like this; in the bottle of a Slovenian-formulated soft drink, or in the words of a book, or in little moments that reminded me of something funny that I wanted to tell him.

The waiter returned without me noticing and I kept my gaze focused on my book.

'It's a perfect day for bananafish, isn't it?' the waiter said. I stopped reading and looked up, caught off guard by what he had said.

He winked at me and pointed to my book saying, 'A favourite of mine.'

'Mine too,' I replied, looking at him. For a moment, I forgot the book entirely. I couldn't help but grin as the young man before me smiled. He reminded me of someone, but I couldn't quite figure out whom. He started to talk about Salinger, about books, about something; I don't know what, because I wasn't quite concentrating. I think I said something in return, but I couldn't for the life of me remember what. There was something about him which made me feel something I hadn't felt in a long time. That funny feeling you get in your stomach. I felt safe, yet excited at the same time.

He finished talking and I smiled back at him. I smiled because I felt happy—*really* happy—a feeling I had almost forgotten.

'My name is Mileva,' I said to him, extending my hand. 'But you can call me Mara, if you like.'

His lips curled upwards slightly at the edges, almost cheekily, as he took my hand and shook it. My hand in his hand felt good, like he wasn't just grabbing it; rather, he was taking it and holding it.

'My name is Saša,' he said, grinning widely and looking straight into my eyes. 'And … is that a Dalmatian accent I detect?'

I couldn't help but laugh a little, in that giggly sort of girlish way that I thought I had outgrown. I looked at this man, Saša, and I realised that he did indeed remind me of someone. There was something in him that I thought had only existed in one other person.

I saw a man with smiling eyes, whose face was kind.

Map

Author's Note

This novel is a work of fiction, but the historical events that transpired were real. The characters and personalities in this book, although fictional, are also inspired by real people, namely, my own family.

The novel's protagonist is part of a generation closer to my parents in age than to me, but her observations and experiences draw largely from my own.

My parents' influence contributed to many of the anecdotes and relationships in the novel. I am forever grateful for the stories they've shared with me and the compassion they've instilled in me.

This story captures just one perspective of the many stories of Former Yugoslavia and is by no means the only representation of Former Yugoslavia and its people.

About the Author

Marija Poljak is a high school teacher in Adelaide, South Australia.

Her family migrated to Australia as refugees from Former Yugoslavia when Marija was a child, but they have always remained very connected to their home country and their culture. Marija's work focuses heavily on her cultural background and questions surrounding identity and belonging.

In between writing and teaching, Marija spends most of her time with her husband, son and daughter.

Acknowledgements

I would like to thank everyone who helped make this novel possible.

To my publisher, Rhiza Edge, for seeing the potential and taking on this deeply personal story. To the editing team and designers, and all the individuals involved. Thank you.

To my family and friends for their support and encouragement. To Jelena, for being there from the start. And to my brother, Marin, for reading it first.

To mama and tata. I am so proud to call you my parents.

And finally, to Bojan. Always, and for everything, thank you.